Published by Andreas Publishing

ISBN 978-1-52288-448-4

Also available as a Kindle ebook
978-1-84396-388-2

A CIP catalogue record for this
work is available from the British Library.

This novel is a work of fiction.
Any resemblance between the characters
it portrays and persons living or dead is
entirely coincidental.

Pre-press production
eBook Versions
27 Old Gloucester Street
London WC1N 3AX
www.ebookversions.com

Dedication

My thanks to my good wife Margaret for her unstinting support. And to David Canning for his proofreading of the final draft.

A
DERRY
TALE

John Boyle

ANDREAS PUBLISHING

The Gas Lady

Some like the smell of petrol. I like the smell of gas. A whiff of it today transports me back in a 'whoosh' thirty years. I'm sitting in our little scullery in Derry peeling potatoes with my mother. We're leaning into one another her head bent towards my head. The only sound is the soft splash of the peeled potatoes dropping into the clear water of a big enamel bucket. Mother's apron smells of the fresh dough from the scone loaves she's just baked.

'Did they put her in jail?' I said.

'Fifteen years in Crumlin Road Prison. 'The mothers' of the dead children wanted her hanged. So did the police.'

'Did you ever put me with her when I was a baby?'

Mother, dropping another potato into the enamel bucket looked up at me. 'Once I did John.'

'Is that why I like the smell of gas?'

Mrs Connelly, whose husband, a bricklayer, had an accident on a building site from which he never recovered. He died in the Northern Road Infirmary. They had no children. Destitute she now took in the neighbourhood's ironing. She'd bought a new, top-of-the range, Morphy-Richards gas iron with the small payout from an insurance policy she'd taken out on her husband. Her business thrived. She kept her prices low her ironing quality high. Soon her living room was stacked with clothes

All her neighbours thought highly of her ironing skills and were sympathetic to her plight after the death of her husband. She was now making good steady money. More than given to her by her late bricklaying husband as housekeeping. He'd spent most of his wages in the pub.

Asked by one of her pregnant customers if she'd look after her other three babies while she had the next, she agreed for a small fee. This was the start of another successful little business venture. Soon her home was filled with babies as well as ironing.

It wasn't long before Mrs Connelly found out that the ironing was three times as profitable as baby watching. And less time consuming. And a lot less aggravation. Ironing didn't scream and wail its head off or need its nappy changing. Having worked out a plan of action, she put it into effect.

Now when a mother called to pick up her baby, she'd be delighted to see it contentedly fast asleep. As were all the babies. Turned out in the end that all the contentedly sleeping babies were sleeping under the influence of a whiff of gas given to them soon after their arrival.

A thin flexible tube connected to the gas tap did the trick. And once a new arrival was sleeping soundly, Connelly connected the gas iron up to the same tap and carried on ironing. As she was always ironing when mothers called to pick up their babies, they never thought to ask about the smell of gas. It was always only a whiff as she sensibly kept her parlour window open.

'How'd she get found out?' I said.

'She 'slipped up' and overdosed two of the babies. They both died.'

In those days, of course, the fifties, there were so many babies about in general – and particularly in our little house when father was away in Wales and my then married sisters piled in with their broods – that a 'slip up' was thought of as almost a term of endearment at the death of one.

As a child I slept in a big drop side wooden crafted by father, a shipwright and cabinetmaker, until I was six, here on the ground-floor front room that overlooked the Buncrana Road, in Derry, with my mother and father. They slept in a manufactured bed settee. Mother called this 'front room' of our little rented home, the parlour.

The parlour had two fishtailed gas mantel lights that made a 'whoosh' as father put a match to them. I loved that little 'whoosh' and the lingering smell of gas, so distinct from all the other domestic sounds and smells of our overcrowded little home.

Mother invited into this parlour, the rent collector, insurance man, parish priest, and the 'first footer' on New Year's Eve. All those in fact who called at our front door. Including, much later, prospective boyfriends of my sisters. These included Americans servicemen from Springtown Camp further up the Buncrana Road towards the Irish 'Free State'.

Mother proudly presented herself and family to the world in this immaculately kept parlour. None of us ever came into our home, or left through it, by the front door. If we did, we brought bad luck into the house with us. The 'first footer' brought in good luck.

I saw my reflection in the twice-weekly polished tongue and grooved floorboards in this parlour. Tongue and grooved floorboards that later as an apprentice joiner, I had to on my hands and knees scuff with a smoothing plane. (Hence my 'Joiners' Knee') This to present a flat surface to the polished linoleum which would tear on any slightly raised surface of the floorboards. Wall to wall carpets were unheard of.

There was a shiny veneered-oak press sitting on a

threadbare thin mat, two cushioned second-hand armchairs with sides like wings. I remember falling asleep on one of these 'winged' armchairs. I slept soundly and comfortably. Mother polished the iron coal fireplace and the iron fender weekly with black lead and emery paper. The red-tiled hearth gleamed and sparkled. This fireplace never saw a coal fire from one year's end to the next.

The only time I ever remember it lit was when mother lay ill once on the bed settee, that she and father spent their married life. And in which I spent many a happy night with her. Only later to be so ignominiously exiled, at the tender age of three years, and ensconced in my sisters' upstairs bedroom.

When I was a very young child mother kept my cot alongside her at night. When I started bawling she'd drop the side of my cot and swish me out into her big warm bed. I'd snuggle up to her and, mostly, fall asleep.

When I was three mother put my cot at the bottom of the bed settee and away from her side of the bed. 'You're a big boy now,' she said, 'and big boys don't cry to get into their mother's bed.'

That mother now saw me, as a 'big boy' was way no consolation for this gross injustice. Before I could muster a protest, she followed up with her Cu de grace. 'You're too heavy now for me to lift as well.'

'I'm sorry I'm too heavy for you mummy.'

One Monday night as bedtime came and the girls made their way upstairs, I was wondering why I wasn't in my cot in mother's bedroom, albeit at the bottom of her big bed. 'You're staying up a bit later tonight John, let your sisters get settled in bed first before you go,' mother said.

This was different. I was always in my cot in mother's parlour bedroom before the girls went to their beds. This difference piggybacked over to team up with other differences

I'd noticed of late about mother. She was getting fat. And had the cheek to now tell me *I* was too heavy.

She'd begun to moan and groan in the night as well. I heard her as I lay awake scheming as to how I could best get in beside her and into that great big warm bed of hers. Now there was a huge enamel basin alongside mother where my cot used to be. And father had made good headway on the makings of another cot. Just like the one I was in.

'Daddy I don't *needed* another cot,' I told him. Why are you making me another one?' He tousled my hair, stroked my cheek with his rough hand, and smiled. He was a man of few words. Reticent to the point that smoke signals were loud mouthed by comparison. He did his talking with the tools of his trade. And this language was to me a whole new sweetness, like mother's milk. Not that I'd tasted much of that lately. Another 'big boy' thing apparently.

When making a cot father also always made a kite. This from the tongue and grooved boards used for the bottom of the cot. He'd saw off the 'tongue' part. Make a cross and glue four diagonal pieces to this cross to form a diamond shape. Then tie a piece of string at the bottom, fold small pieces of newspaper into seven or eight 'tabby bows', and attach them to the string. He'd glue newspaper over the frame and attach a long piece of string to the front of the kite. When we had a bit of wind, he'd launch the kite up into the sky from the back yard, diving and swooping about and above the rooftops

'Can I have a go daddy,' the girls would shout, as they danced around in a tight bunch laughing and reaching out for the string. He'd let them all have a go.

He handed the kite to me once. I wrapped the string around my hand and held on. Looking up at the kite as it swooped and dived in the wind I tripped and fell letting the string go. Up, up the kite flew, away above the tops of the houses, towering up into the clouds until I couldn't see it any longer. I glanced up at father. He tousled my hair and laughed.

'I'll make another when I make the next cot,' he said.

What did that mean, when he made the next cot? He was already making one. He'd had a workbench in our little scullery in the winter, re-located in the back yard in the summer months.

Two rough-sawn planks, eighteen inches apart, with a piece of plywood fixed underneath. This is where his tools lay as he worked keeping them below the level of his work piece. Two timber trestles give the needed support. Father did 'foreigners' (work outside his day job) for others, working at weekends and evenings to supplement his pittance of a weekly wage. And to pay for all the timber he used making all manner of wooden things for us and our home.

These included cots, yes, but at Christmastime, he made wooden toys. A wooden train, on six wheels made from thread spools sawn in half, three spools, six wheels, with a tender full of different sized hardwood blocks for fuel, a thin multi-coloured rope to shunt it along.

A square wooden Douglas Fir box filled with different sizes and shapes of wooden blocks that you could place together to make further shapes. And a hen, speckled with sawdust keeps in place with animal glue, shaped out of a single piece of hardwood, and fixed to a platform with four wheels.

Like the cots, none of these wooden toys was painted or varnished, father leaving them in their bare, silky innocence. The fact that neither the cots, nor the wooden toys, were painted or varnished made plain their hand-made rather than manufactured, origin.

These toys passed down from child to child, just like our clothes. I remember the soft scent and prolonged clean sound of his smoothing plane dressing the wood to a glossy silkiness. The thin shavings curling into elegant little bangles as they floated down to the cold, uncomprehending, concrete of the scullery floor.

The honest buzz and burr of his hand saw cutting through seasoned wood with a cheese-wire exactness, little blizzards of sawdust sinking and gathering on the floor and floating in the air making me sneeze and rub my nose. A habit I still have to this day. I'll rub my nose and sneeze for a week.

The rotten-egg smell of pellets of animal glue melting into a liquid on the gleaming black-lead polished range. When sawing he always kept his thumb pressed lightly against the blade of his 'Disston' saw. Distracted once he nicked his thumb. Blood slow motioned into the sawdust below thickening it into a little mealy paste. He wetly licked his thumb. Stooped, causally down, and pressed it, still bleeding, into this paste and kept it there for a little. Picked up his saw and carried on.

Anyway, that Monday night, when I should have been on my cot in mother's bedroom, my sisters already in bed for sometime, I fell asleep. Mother picked me up. 'Time for beddy byes John,' she said.

Instead of turning left into the parlour, she climbed the stairs. 'I've moved you in with Gerty, Bridy, and Ann. Just for a little while. I've things to attend to.' she said.

Things to attend to. What did that mean?

Gerty was the eldest of the girls. Then came Bridget, Phyllis, Maureen, Angelia, and Eleanor, all older than me. Then after me, the first boy, Michael, then Frank, my two brothers, and last my sister, Bernadette. There was but a year and a half to two years between any two of us.

All three sisters were already in bed my cot at a right angle to theirs. As soon as mother put me in my cot, I started to bawl. I was only three. But I knew how effective bawling

7

was in getting me into mother's big soft bed. Even though it didn't work now with her quite as easily as before. But this was only because she clearly wasn't at herself.

'Shss, shss,' mother said. You'll wake the girls'.

But I could see and hear they were only pretending to be asleep, as little giggles and snorts escaped from their partially closed mouths. Their eyes closed tight. Too tight. I wasn't impressed with this new arrangement. Even thought my sisters, mostly Ann, did get up from time to time to tuck and tousle me in and make a bit of fuss.

After three years the novelty of a boy in the house had worn thin with my sisters. Except for Ann. Now mother introduced another boy novelty by planting me in my sisters' bedroom without a by-your-leave. I knew that this tucking and tousling from my sisters wouldn't last long. It was just the novelty of having me in their bedroom that made them so nice to me. I knew that.

One night I lay awake waiting for the girls to go asleep. This took hours. They could talk those sisters of mine. Endlessly. And about absolutely nothing that I found even remotely interesting.

'Did you see the look on Joe Ferry's face when I told him to get lost after he tried to put his arm around my waist and cuddle me,' said Gerty, the eldest who slept in the single bed. My younger sisters were in thrall to Grety. They both giggled and clapped at this.

'And what'll you do for him tomorrow if he does it again?' said Bridy. This is what I was to endure every night of the week. After about eleven hours, they fell asleep.

Having clocked mother doing it, I unclipped one side, then the other of the drop-down section of my cot and quietly lowered it to the floor. The rungs on the drop side were horizontal for added strength. I inched my way backward gripping on to the top rail. Inched is right, as I feared toppling the cot over and breaking a leg or something.

Not that breaking a leg meant much to me at three years of age. But waking up my three sisters would've been worse. Of that I was sure. As my feet touched the floor, I felt my head spin a little. I just shook it once or twice and carried on.

A full moon hung in the curtainless window as I tiptoed across the landing to the stairs proper. The wind moaned— it sounded a bit like mother's moan— rattling the window sash in its frame. The rain-wet roofs of the houses backing onto ours, Saint Bridget's Avenue, were gleaming and sparkling under the dazzle of the full moon. The dim light under the over-hanging roof's eaves cast its frowning shadow at me.

The near side of St Patrick's chapel hung radiant in the sash. The saints in their stained glass windows, robes bathed in the purity of the innocent moonlight, blazed like a summer's sun at noon.

And the saints weren't just in the stained glass windows but all around me on every side; St. Patricks Terrace, St Bridget's Avenue, St. Francis's Terrace...' They were in my blood, my head. Maybe that's why my head went dizzy when I inched out of my cot and my feet touched the floor.

The moon shone me to the bottom of the stairs. Right to the hall coat- hanger stand opposite the parlour door behind which mother and father slept. I nearly stepped into the enamel basin at the side of her bed. It was empty. I climbed in beside her. She was as warm as a big pork pie.

'What are you doing?' You should be in your cot. Your freezing,' she said as I put my feet on her. She pulled me into her for a moment. A moment's right. 'You'll have to stay in your cot in your sister's room,' she said.

'Why?'

'Shss shss', mother said. Because after a certain age it's not healthy. It's better you sleeping on your own when

9

you're the age you are.'

'That's all right,' I said. I don't care if I catch a cold.'

'That's not what I meant.' Anyway, she said, you'll wake your father, he's got to be up early for work. Then the coup de grace again.' And you know, I'm not... well. I've things to get ready for.'

What did all this mean?

'Are you going to be sick again?' There was no reply to this. I thought I was in. I said, 'But I like sleeping with you and father in the parlour'. I was trying desperately to impress her with my use of the word ' parlour', that I'd heard her use; "I'll see the insurance man, priest... in the parlour."

But all this inveigling was in vain. Mother eased me onto the floor. And groaning and sighing, she lifted herself out of bed, grabbed me by the hand and we traipsed back up the stairs she all the while holding tightly onto my hand. In between groaning, she continued to say, 'Shss, shss', as I tried to explain that I didn't like being in my sister's bedroom. God, how I hated that 'Shss', 'shss.' 'Who lowered your cot side?' mother said. Was it Ann?'

I pretended not to understand and said nothing.

Mother knew Ann had a special fondness for me. So she drilled into Ann the following day that it was up to her to make sure I didn't leave my cot again during the night. I, innocently, of course, didn't know why the leaving of my cot to get into my mother's big warm bed was such a big deal in the first place. Still, what does a three-year old boy know?

My sisters, girls that they were, did. Girls always need to know these things before boys Ann told me. What did *that* mean? Anyway, I languished in my cot for an inconsolable number of nights listening to inane, endless, but now whispering chatter.

Ann always woke me each morning. But his morning she didn't, I woke myself. 'Why didn't you wake me?' She turned around, gathered me out of my cot tousling my drowsy head and stroking my cheek with her soft hand.

'It's a special day today,' she said. We're off up to see your uncle Fred in 'The Glen'. Uncle Fred was married to my mother's sister, my aunt Annie. 'And your aunt Annie's down stairs with mother in the front room.'

This was more puzzling than why mother wouldn't allow me into her big bed under this nonsense that I was now a 'big boy'. I didn't *feel* like a big boy. I was only three.

But clear to me at least was the fact that the main reason mother didn't want me to be in her big warm bed was that she just wasn't at herself. And that when she came to herself again, I was certain I'd be back in bed with her.

Father, who was always at work by this time, sat by himself at the breakfast table that was a clutter of plates of half-eaten porridge. He wasn't in his work clothes. He'd on a white simmet, thin shapeless, creased dark trousers. His feet were bare. And he hadn't shaved. He was always clean-shaven. Why was he in his bare feet?

The kitchen was warm and cosy with the range fire blazing, timber sparking, coal flaring and 'whooshing' as the gas escaped from its enclosed black case. A big hessian bag of short ends of timber, father had brought home from his work, lay to one side of the range. The big swan spout of the black kettle billowed gouts of steam, spitting out water that griddled and skittered on the red-hot lid of the range. Our cat stood under the table, his back bristling, meowing, his saucer milkless.

'You both can have your breakfast up at your uncle Fred's,' father said. Your aunt Annie's in with your mother now.'

What was Aunt Annie doing in mother's bedroom?

I took a shufty out the scullery to see a stranger in a priest-white long- sleeved shirt, rolled up at the cuffs, leaning

11

into our Belfast sink. He was washing his big soft hands in Fairy soap-sudsy warm water from the kettle on the range that steamed up the little window above the sink. He looked at me and winked with one of his big sky-blue eyes, then carried on washing and scrubbing.

On the hall coat-hanger stand lay a big worn creased purse, its mouth gaping wide.

The interior soft with crinkly velvet, like the velvet curtains in mother's front room, curtsey of St. Vincent de Paul. Black tubes with silver endings hung out of this purse. A long overcoat, the colour of dark treacle, with a shiny fur-like collar hung on one of the hallstand hooks. A pair of black leather gloves drooped out of one of the big pockets. Not the kind of coat you'd see used as bed covering, leastways not on a 'Boyle' bed.

'What, where, why...?' I said.

'Shss, shss,' Ann said, tightening her grip on my hand as we hurried toward the front door. That 'Shss, 'shss again. I could hear mother moaning and groaning, only much louder now as we passed the door of her bedroom. I looked back just before Ann opened the front door to see the stranger with the priest-white shirt, cuffs still rolled up, picking up the big open purse, and going into mother's bedroom.

'Why aren't we going out the back?' I said. We never go out the front.' But I was wasting my three year-old sweetness on the desert air.

Ann both lugged and walked me up to 'The Glen' that day.

Uncle Fred, who worked at the Lough Swilly train station sat at a similar range to ours, only it wasn't as shiny. And there wasn't a swan-necked big kettle on it either. He was raking at the coal embers, hunched over in his chair. The handle of the poker polished bright with use, the business end worn to a twisted, tortured point.

'Ah', he said, there you both are. I'll get some porridge on the go for you.'

Uncle Fred was in the house on his own. His two sons, Billy and John, both bricklayers, were working for Du Point, at the Maydown plant in the Waterside at Campsie.

There was one of father's cots in the kitchen. They were everywhere these cots of his. I can't believe I didn't dream about them as well. As it was windy outside I asked uncle Fred if he had a kite I could play with in his back yard to pass the time.

'No, I don't, he said. What make you think I had?'

The walk had tired me out. And after a plate of Uncle Fred's porridge Ann put me in the cot where I slept for hours. It was dark when Ann and I got home. She took me straight to my cot and tucked me in. Grety and Bridy were already in bed but not yet sleeping, as usual. The only usual thing of the day. But they were quiet. When they did speak, as the did now to Ann, it was in conspiratorial whispers.

'How the new...?' Gerty said.

Ann cut her short. 'You'll both know about all that in the morning, now get asleep you're keeping John awake. I'm back off down the stairs. You make sure you stay in your cot John or you'll get me into trouble with mother, and you don't want that now do you?' she said rubbing my warm cheeks with her soft hand.

I couldn't believe Gerty took this without some kind of retort. She was the eldest after all and used to telling Ann and the rest of my sisters what to do.

But she said nothing. It was hard for me to believe that Gerty was asking how the new cot was doing. But what else was new in our house but the new cot. This was all very puzzling for a three year old.

But I didn't ask any questions. I was tired. Anyway, I knew if I did. I'd just get, 'Shss, 'shss'.

I awoke late in the night. In the moonlight that seeped through our thin bedroom curtains I saw that Ann still wasn't in bed. My two sisters were fast asleep.

As Ann wasn't here, I reasoned, why should I be? I eased the drop side of my cot to the floor. And again, inched my way down the rungs. I thought of the saints as my head spun when my feet touched the floor. But I just shook my head and carried on.

Sensibly 'big boy' that I now was, I'd quietly put in a bit of practice climbing down these rungs. And while not having turned it into a fine art, I was, by now, pretty good at it.

So much so that when older and at the school sport of cross-country running, I was always fields ahead of the pack. And the number of fields ahead was determined by how many field gates I had to climb up and down. Here the expertise garnered climbing in and out of my cot as a child, stood me in terrific stead.

And as if to confirm the link between this childhood practice and climbing fields gates, my head always spun as my feet touched the ground. Here again I knew what to do. I just shook my head and carried on.

The moon shinning thorough the curtainless landing window shone me down the stairs again. Thank you moon. There was a strange pungent disinfectant smell. A bit like the smell from the mop bucket after mother had added a drop of amber liquid into the warm water.

All was quiet and still. The purse with its mouth gaping open on the coat- hanger stand was gone. As was the coat. I eased my way into the parlour. The moonlight shone faintly through the thick velvet curtains. (curtsey of Saint Vincent De Paul's) mother and father were fast asleep.

Their bed covers were different. They were pure white, priest white, like the shirt of that stranger in our scullery.

On the short-legged table stood the big white enamel

basin, sodden cotton wool floating in the dark water. Again, that pungent disinfectant smell.

A mangled bar of green Fairy soap lay forlornly in the little delft saucer. From the far corner of the room a faint shadow stirred. It was aunt Annie tucked up in one of the wing chairs with a big overcoat wrapped around her. The universal blanket of the Boyles all over Ireland.

The new cot sat gleaming in its unpolished innocent finery, side dropped and pulled up against mother's side of the bed where it used to be for me when I was not a 'big boy'. Maybe mother's expecting me? Especially with the drop side of the cot already down. I wondered if I should climb into that first. From there mother could swish me into her big warm bed. I puzzled too as to where Ann was.

My eyes now accustomed to the darkness of mother's bedroom, I spotted my sister Ann lying with her head against the wing of the other armchair. She'd a pure white sheet gathered around her. She was snoring lightly. *So, this is where she's been all the time. What's she doing here?*

On seeing father's head was a foot down his pillow, making a clear passage between his big head and the headboard, I give up the idea of clambering into the cot first, where mother could whisk me into to her big warm bed. I started instead to crawl up unto father's pillow.

Mother stirred. I heard a kind of burbling sound as though she was going to be sick again. Then she began to sing. Ever so softly, so as not to wake father who'd have to get up for work in the morning after having had a full day off work for no apparent reason.

'Hush a bye baby, on the tree top, when the wind blows the cradle will rock,' she sang. She knew I was coming. She was singing for me

She is expecting me. I was right about the dropped side of the cot being down. Mother dropped it for me. But it was too late to climb into the cot now. I eased myself between mother, whose back was to me, and father and lay very still, not even breathing, listening, trying to control my excitement at being back in bed with mother.

Father was at the very edge of the bed. His mouth open, snoring softly, his lips puckering in and out with each breath. His inward snore sounded different from his out. His 'out' like the sonar 'ping' of the submarine in the film 'Run Silent, Run Deep' that I later watched with mother in the 'Odeon' picture house on the Strand Road. He still hadn't had a shave.

In trying to control my excitement, as best as a three year old could, my cold feet touched father's legs.

'My God Mary,' he said, turning and making full contact with me, 'the child's freezing.' Then; 'My God he's grown quickly.'

'Shss, shss,' mother said. That 'Shss', 'shss', again, I've been hearing it all my life. Now mother was saying it to father. 'He's here now', let him stay'.

Mother reached into the cot. Then she turned to face me as I turned to her.

'What do think of the new wee baby Dr O'Donnell brought for us all when you were up at your uncle Fred's?' she said in a voice of hoarsened triumph

At mother's 'Shssing', and father's raised voice, Ann, and my aunt Annie, woke. Ann tweaked open a little one of the heavy velvet curtains. Dawn light seeped into mother's bedroom, like split ink slow motioning across blotting paper, whiting the white sheet reefed around Ann and the white pristine sheets on mother's bed.

Now there were four of us in mother's bed. Everyone was awake but the new baby, tucked into mother who'd lifted him (a 'him' as it turned out) from the new cot, just as she used to lift me from my cot. I never remembered her singing to me. And I was sure that the new wee baby wouldn't either.

Ann came to father's side of the bed and reached over. 'Come on John, you go back in your cot upstairs.' I didn't want mother to blame Ann for my being in the bed. I put my arms up ready for Ann to lift me out.

Before Ann could do this, mother said, 'it's all right Ann, 'It's not your fault. It's all right, John can stay. He just wants to look at the new wee baby.'

'What are you like?' Ann said to me, smiling.

As if on cue everyone started to laugh. Including father. Not loud. A kind of chuckling each turning to look at the other. I listened, spellbound. I felt part of this chuckling, it wrapped itself around me like a warm cosy robe. The new wee baby slept through it all.

In later years I watched mother dying in this bed. Dr O'Donnell, his stethoscope dangling from his neck in attendance again, but this time not for a birth, but a death. And Father Glackin in a purple stole going full pelt with prayers for the dying. Some answered, while others' were crying.

I stood alongside father, whose head was bent down to mother, speaking softly, calling her 'girl' and 'love...' Then; 'I'm sorry Mary, I'm sorry,' he said.

But, she couldn't hear him. She lay there, her eyes unblinking, her thin, mottled hands scrabbling at the white pristine bed sheets.

Dr. O'Donnell, catching my eye, winked me over with his now bloodshot big blue eye. 'This's a prescription for your mother, there's a chemist open in Messines Park.' The raw smell of alcohol from his breath stung my eyes.

His face, fattened out now, purpled, and red veined, eyes opaque and lifeless, mirroring the suffering he sees all around him on a daily basis. He handed me the prescription. I stopped crying, wiping my eyes with my cuff. I hared of to the chemist, as Father Glackin was anointing mother. When

I got back she was dead. The prescription was for throat lozenges

Frank, then Bernadette followed Michael. An unending stream of births, cots, and kites. And all in a two-up-and two-down terraced house. Although father had converted both upstairs bedrooms into four small ones.

Like me Michael, Frank, Bernadette, and my sisters before me, all had new cots made for them. They all slept in these until they were six or seven. All these handcrafted robust cots father sold or exchanged for mattressless double and single bed frames.

St. Vincent de Paul supplied the mattresses, stained, and filled with what looked like reddish wire wool bursting out all over. And from which a peculiar, faintly recognisable disinfectant smell arose.

Later, when I discovered the game 'musical chairs', I thought of our' musical cots.' One old cot moving out and one new cot moving in with another new occupant.

This time Michael, whom mother was singing too, when I thought, or wished, she was singing to me. He, too, would have to suffer the indignity, as I did, of hearing mother saying, 'you're a big boy now, and big boys don't cry to get into their mother's bed.'

But he wouldn't, now, have to suffer a whiff of gas from a flexible tube connected to a gas tap in Mrs Connelly's parlour.

Aunt Gertrude

How I spoke was something I'd grown up feeling ashamed of. A shame re-enforced by the plumy, tyrannical accents of the BBC presenters that we listened to after father brought home our first radio.

The 'Mc Cooeys', broadcast on the BBC Radio Ulster in the fifties, was an on-going series about the lives and loves of a Belfast family. And how they spoke was the other end of this language spectrum. Here, all the characters spoke with a pronounced, broad Northern Irish accent. The accent of the Scottish Planter, raucous, quick, abrupt with vowels and consonants crashing into and ricocheting off one another.

The Derry accent is similar, influenced as it is by this Scottish Planter raucousness. But softer, less abrupt, more measured, still maintaining, as it does, the lyrical hint of the indigenous Irish.

But mother saw enough resemblance, as between how we all spoke, and how the McCooey's spoke, that it brought a grimaced look of disgust to her face. 'Turn that off,' she pleaded with father. 'Voices like that shouldn't be allowed on the radio.'

This look of disgust, desperation even, so apparent on mother's face and in conjunction with the plumy voices of the BBC announcers, incubated feelings of inferiority in us children as to how we sounded when we spoke. And these feelings of inferiority were further enforced when we heard said, 'that those from Protestant schools spoke better than those from the Catholic schools.'

To boot, our aunt Gertrude, rubbed salt into this linguistic wound every Saturday evening with her garbled attempt to disguise this 'disgusting' accent, which mother found so unbearable in the McCooey's on Radio Ulster.

Our childless aunt Gertrude, father's sister, lived alone. She'd been left a sum of money, no one knew just how much, by an elderly couple, Mr. & Mrs. McDivvit, whom she'd cared for until they died.

After this she started to visit us early on Saturday evening. I didn't know she existed up until then. Mother told me she found this sudden desire of our aunt's to come and visit us puzzling. But the soul of discretion that she was, said nothing

The McDivvits had lived in a big house off the Culmore Road, Boom Hall. Our aunt had cycled there and back each day. A two mile round journey. This private road was unmade, except for a thin layer of broken stone. In the high winds of October and on into March it was often blocked by fallen trees over which our aunt would drag herself and her bicycle. She sensibly carried a puncture kit.

She bought her home, 14 Argyle Street, just off the Northern Road, up from the red-bricked McGee College. In later years she would be besieged with pleas from my then married sisters to come and stay with her as they couldn't find anywhere to live other than in their parents' homes. Something father turned his back on when asked by his married daughters

But when father went to Wales, to work on the Trawsfynydd nuclear power station, my married sisters all piled in with their children into our little home.

Our aunt's nagging advice mother said, she could put up with. 'That old-fashioned range,' I'd heard her say to mother, 'it's a thing of the past. It's time you got a new tiled fireplace. Everyone has them now. Your sister Annie's sons are bricklayers, they can help your John put it in.' But it was our aunt's attempt at a more refined accent that really spooked mother.

She's your father's sister,' mother would say by way of mitigation. 'We're all entitled to our little ways.'

We'd a lead-blackened coal fire range in the kitchen. This is where mother did all the cooking and the heating of water for bathing. A small scullery with a Belfast sink for the washing of dishes, where food in general was prepared, and all utensils and crockery kept.

The scullery door lead under the stairs where father kept endless pieces of scrap timber. He'd work these scrap pieces of timber into silken wooden toys. At Christmastime dead un-plucked poultry hung by their stretched necks from this door. There was no bathroom.

This Saturday visit by our aunt was a momentous event for the whole family. Especially for mother who was mad keen to show her family and her home off in the best possible light. Preparations for her visit began early.

Our standard outside lavatory stood forlornly at the bottom of the part concrete, part dirt clay, back yard, its door, a foot of the ground, facing into the yard with six two-inch holes spaced out evenly along its top. The braced, ledged, and sheeted back gate leading to the back lane was to its right.

Green gloss paint covered our lavatory door and back gate. As it did all the lavatories doors and back gates of our neighbours. This paint a good-will gesture from the Americans sailors at the Springtown camp just off the

21

Buncrana Road. As a child it never crossed my mind that this good-will gesture may have had an ulterior motive. And this ulterior motive surfaced later when asked by an American sailor if I'd any sisters.

We all of us used the back lane to come and go. Neighbour visiting neighbour used this dirt-clay back lane.

Here the Brock men collected the household slops for their pigs, including all potato peelings. And drunken men late on a Saturday night could be heard arguing, singing and sometimes fighting. This before they slipped in home through their back gates, where the arguing, singing and fighting sometimes started all over again. Father's face would grimace in disgust at this. He'd no time for these 'tossers' as he called them.

He'd taken the pledge. And had never drunk alcohol in his life. Except on two occasions. After the murder of his son. And on his deathbed. Where, with a wink and a weak nod of his head, he beckoned me over.

'For Christ's sake John, will you get me a glass of whiskey.' I've had about enough of listening to this 'tosser' Glackin.' Father Glackin, who was going hammer and tongs at the prayers for the dying, stopped when he heard this.

I shot across the road to the 'Collon Bar'. 'Whiskey for the 'Oldman,' I said to Raymond the bartender.

'He's not going to make it then John?' he said, as he handed me a quarter bottle of 'Bush Mill's' whiskey. I didn't know he drank. 'I thought he'd taken the 'pledge.'

I hared back. Unscrewed the top, handed the whiskey to father. He put the bottle to his lips, spat it out. 'God Almighty, people drink this stuff.' The bottle dropped from his hand spilling its content onto the faded tasselled rug, the smell stinging my nostrils. Father Glackin revved up again pelting away at the prayers for the dying.

People shoaled up and down our back lane all the time.

And especially on a Sunday and 'holy days of obligation' on their way to Mass. Or, a funeral.

After Mass, it thronged with small groups of quiet intense stone-faced men. Some squatting at their card schools others standing in tight bunches at their 'pitch and toss' schools. 'Along its 'heathen length' as mother said of our back lane on Sunday. She later extended 'along it's heathen length' on a Sunday to every day of the week.

When later the boyfriends of my sisters called at our front door, they were met by father. He'd give them a good coat of looking over and have them wait until properly invited into the parlour by the mother. This invitation only offered upon their making heart-felt representations to mother as to their feelings for one of her daughters.

Now on Saturday afternoon, instead of the usual Friday, mother enthroned on our out-side lavatory, door wide open, would preach the benefits of we children stomping up and down, bare-legged and footed, on the week's wash in our big tin bath, enthroned, like mother on the 'loo', in our back yard. As each Saturday loomed mother saw this as an important preparation for the impending visit of our aunt that evening. And another opportunity to impress our father's sister.

The six girls had a go first, three at a time. After the six girls had had a go of stomping up and down on the week's wash it was our boys' turn. Mother would shout, 'Right girls out, let your brothers in.' In we'd go splashing and laughing, pushing and shoving and being pushed and shoved back in turn.

The girls would dance around the bath laughing clapping and shouting. All of our heads spinning as we collectively became one sucked up into a noisy vortex of our own glorious making.

'Your feet'll be spotless, a week's wash done,' mother would intone, urging us on to greater stomping vigour as she sat, unabashed on our outside lavatory. 'Your aunt will be proud of us all.' Bernie, my youngest sister, with a little smile on her bright face, stood alongside mother.

And every Wednesday we had a special wash for our aunt's visit. Old overcoats, curtsey of 'Saint Vincent De Paul', the major clothier of poor families for the city of Derry and its environs.Saint Vincent De Paul had warehouses full of all kinds of second-hand clothes, shoes, boots, bedding, mattresses, donated, in the main, by better off Catholics. If he'd still been alive, he'd have had his pious hands full in Derry and its environs in the early 1950's.

Father had made five narrow, deep, wooded boxes to keep the various items that made up all the bed coverings. One for mother and him, and one each of the upstairs bedrooms. Bernie was still in her cot in mother and father's parlour bedroom. Father called these boxes Saint Vincent de Paul boxes. 'Mother always smiled wryly at this.

The next preparatory step for the impending visit of our aunt was our weekly bath in the kitchen. A weekly bath time now re-scheduled for Saturday afternoons to suit her visit. The same set up as the weekly clothes wash, girls first, three at a time.

The fire would be blazing in the range. Coals hissing and firing out little streams of smoke and flames. The big tin bath full of warm soapy water, heated on the daily lead-polished coal- fired iron range in the huge blackened kettle. Its spout a giant black swan's neck. Mother had to use both hands to lift it on and off the red-hot lid of the range after dragging it in from the scullery, the only place we had a water tap.

Anchored by the bath stood mother. She'd a large tattered towel over her right shoulder and a white flannel 'face cloth' gripped in her hand. Her jet-black hair now flecked with grey, curtaining out beyond her reddening cheeks and falling onto her brow as she got ready for the onslaught.

A mangled green bar of Fairy soap innocently lying in a sudsy delft saucer on a small pine table, its grain raised with the soapy water. The oil-clothed floor of the kitchen was awash and slippery with sudsy water. Mother from time to time, moped this up with an old-fashioned rope mop and tin perforated bucket.

Michael, Frank, and I stood on the landing listening to the squeals and laughter of the girls, hearing the warm soapy water sloshing against the tin bath, splashing out onto the linoleum covering the cement floor. The admonishing, cries of mother echoed up to us.

The roar of the blazing coal and timber fire added further music to our impatient ears and the smell of the hot, sweet soapy water filling our nostrils. We'd stomped about the landing with the same vigour that we'd stomp on the weekly wash, waiting our turn, tearing down the stairs as the second trio of girls tore past us giggling and laughing on all fronts. Father, went for a long walk around the 'Branch' during these extended ablutions.

Mother now and again, drew water from the main bath, pouring it into a smaller tin bath in the scullery. Undergarments were then washed in this bath. She'd then add more hot water from the big kettle to the main bath. Soapy suds disguised the colour of the water. We'd get through two or three of these big tin baths ever year and twenty three bars of 'Fairy' soap.

Directly across from our home was the Lough Swilly railway line. As the steam train, huffing, puffing, whistling, thundered by on its way to the holiday resort of Buncrana in Donegal, the reverberation sends shivers across both the bath water and us.

The deafening harshness of the steam train's whistle,

the roar of the steam engine, belching out its smoke signals drowned out all other sounds. We, all of us stood stock still until it passed as though in acknowledgement of another more harsh and unforgiving world waiting for us beyond our little home here in Saint Patricks Terrace.

I was three years old when first I went to Buncrana for the day with my sisters, Gerty, Bridy, and Phyllis. We walked to the Lough Swilly Train station, where uncle Fred worked, the sun blistering the tarmac road. The steam train was full to the gunwales with day-trippers intent on spending a day on the beach. I sat on Gerty's lap.

I'd never seen ribbed sand before. Nor crashing waves, nor so much water. Running along the beach on this ribbed, damp solid sand, I stopped and looked back. I'd left my footprints behind me. I bent down and pressed my hands into the sand. I'd left my hand prints in it.

I was Robinson Crusoe, cast away on a deserted Island, and stumbling across the footprints of 'Man Friday'. But these were my footprints. Not someone else's. I'd changed the earth I'd walked on. And was now master of it. Something of me was now outside of me.

I hared down to the water's edge, the waves slamming into the shelved shore, water flooding up the beach and over my bare feet. I looked defiantly out at the Atlantic Ocean and felt that if I wanted to I could stop the waves in their tracks. Like King Canute.

I ran towards the thundering waves. But they kept coming. I sensibly beat a hasty retreat, falling over, exhausted, exhilarated, my head light and spinning like a flung coin flicked into the air, by the 'pitch and 'toss' players.

... It was seventeen years on when next I went to Buncrana. And this visit, of a week, was also a kind of epiphany for me. I stayed in St. Bridget's boarding house in the main street. The only others staying there were two Nuns, on sabbatical, according to the landlady. I saw one of them at breakfast.

This time I was on my own. It was late autumn. The town was quiet. As was the beach where I'd first run across the ribbed sea sand as a three year old. Each morning, before breakfast, I'd walk along this beach inhaling the salty spray of the North Atlantic Ocean. Sometimes breaking into a run as I did as a child, and looking back now at my bigger, deeper footprints.

On the last morning of my stay the weather was cloudy with a weak sun glinting off the traffic-light green sea. In the distance I spotted a lone figure dressed in a long black gown standing at the sea's edge.

As I moved up the beach, I could see it was a Nun. It wasn't the Nun I'd seen at the breakfast table. It must be the other one. She didn't see me as I approached. Her feet were bare. Her black veil swung in the stiffing breeze. The sun grew weaker, sheltering behind thickening cloud.

She was holding in her right hand and out in front of her a glass chalice filled with a reddish liquid. Her head slumped onto her chest as though in contemplation. It reminded me of Father Glackens's slumped head as he waited for the wailing children to stop wailing at Mass that Sunday.

I stopped maybe fifty yards away. She slowly raised her head, looking out to sea.

Her right hand now elevated, the chalice in line with her raised head, she started to sing. Her voice rang out clear as a hammer striking an anvil, out over the great green go-light of the harsh Atlantic Ocean. Up out of the waters, seals with horse-like heads appeared.

Light gathered in the reddish liquid of her glass chalice. In they came to congregate around her in their silver-grey finery, one flipper raised out of the water as though in acknowledgement of her presence and voice. She sang for

27

about five minutes to this mesmerised congregation. Then she stopped. Lowering her right hand, she put the chalice to her mouth. Spat it out.

She poured the remaining reddish liquid into the ribbed sand. Flung the chalice out into the Ocean. Slowly each seal departed its watery pew. Back to the deep green go-light of the sea from whence they had come. There to await the next coming.

But the next coming was on its way. Slowly the Nun entered the water as though to follow the seals. I watched now from twenty yards. She kept on wading out into the sea. The water was at her shoulders as I tore up the beach. I shouted. She turned around slowly in the heaving water. Looked at me straight on and swayed her head from side to side then disappeared under the vengeful North Atlantic Ocean. Before her head sunk below the waves I saw a long white scar on her upper lip.

I left on the bus for Derry the next day. The days of the Lough Swilly trains only a distance memory. Seals, Nuns, foot and hand print all wrestling for space in my dizzy, spinning head.

At one point, opposite our home, the Lough Swilly railway track crossed a small stream on its way to the river Foyle. To get across it I had to speel over one of the railway tracks, my feet just clear of the water. I slipped. My first front teeth came down with a crunch onto the iron track. Reaching the other side I saw these two front teeth lying on the track in a little pool of blood and spittle.

A slight breeze stiffened and blew my two teeth into the stream. I watched as they tumbled away in the clear water on their way to the darker water of the river Foyle and on out into the antediluvian soil of the North Atlantic Ocean.

In this same small stream my brother Michael and I used

to wash the black earth from the roots of shamrocks three or four days before St. Patrick's Day. We sat on a broad plank of timber that straddled the stream. We'd dangle our bare feet in the clear tumbling water, leaning down into it washing the shamrock roots.

Sometimes a bunch of shamrocks slipped from our hands and bustled off down stream. A net five yards downstream caught such slipped bunches. Fred McGilloway, a fisherman, paid us a miserly penny for every twenty bunches washed.

With me keeping scout for McGilloway, Michael splashed down this stream, lifted the net as I dumped bunches of shamrocks that sailed under it. Further downstream, Frank, my other brother, waited. We later sold these shamrocks to neighbours. We had a three-way split of the proceeds. We were as 'thick as thieves' my two brothers and me.

Once bathed, one of many preparation for the Saturday visit by our aunt, clothes donned, upstairs we went, knowing what was coming next.

And what was coming next? The dreaded weekly 'Senna Pods'. We'd all scatter, hiding under beds, some of us in the one wardrobe, others in bed hiding under the 'blankets' as soon as we heard mother's first footfall on the stairs.

'Right, so you don't want any 'Sharp toffees' this evening.'

OK,' she'd say, pretending to make her way back downstairs. All we children knew that the great joy of our aunt's visit, for us, was one of the two big brown paper bags she brought with her.

One of these paper bags was full of plums. None of us children knew at first sight what they were, not having seen anything as exotic as a plum before. But when father placed them in a clear glass dish on the sideboard they looked like white-powered, purple globes pulsating with sweetness and promise. They brought saliva to each of our mouths. The plums were for mother and father.

The other brown paper bag was full of small clear bags of toffees. It was these toffees mother used as an inducement on a Saturday morning for us to take our 'Senna pods'. All the toffees were for us children.

We'd all line up in a grumbling, raggedy line. One elbowing the other to secure a place at the back. We'd be screwing up our faces at the foul smell and taste ladled into our mouths with a large spoon used exclusively for this purpose. It felt like ritualised torture. And especially so after the fun and games of bathing in the big tin bath in front of a blazing, hissing coal fire. There were cast -iron fireplaces in the upstairs bedrooms. But their grates never saw any coal never mind a fire. The range was king.

Every Saturday morning after the dreaded 'Senna Pods', all the bed and cot mattresses were sprayed with DDT.

'Good night, good night', mother would recite at bedtime, 'don't let the bed bugs bit'. But DDT or not they still continued to bite.

We all of us stayed at home on Saturday evenings. But later the strain inflicted on mother by these visits from our constantly nagging aunt morphed into mother and me going to the pictures on a Saturday evening. Our aunt was always gone by the time mother and I got home.

I remember a Second World War film that frightened me because it was all actually happening. The screaming German 'Messerschmitt' planes, coming in low, strafing refugees streaming along a highway. Bullets ploughing into the earth and people. Men, women and children flinging themselves into roadside ditches. Handcarts full of their raggedy possessions...

'Why do they do that mummy?' I could see tears in her eyes. 'Why don't we go home mummy?' I said, tugging at her sleeve.

She blew her nose. Man's inhumanity to man makes countless millions weep,' she said.

'What does inhumanity mean?' I said.

Coming home from the pictures one Saturday, mother and I heard voices as we came into our back lane. A policeman had a man up against the wall, his hand around his throat. Another policeman had his drawn baton dangling by his side. 'You'll need to give us more than that', the policeman with his hand around the man's throat said as he crashed his booted foot down on the man's instep.

'For Christ's sake', the man said.' I don't know any...'

The man had seen mother and me. The two policemen turned and saw us as well.

The one with the drawn baton smashed it sideways across the man's ear. He fell to the ground clutching at his destroyed ear. The policemen ambled off down our lane. 'How's the family?' one said to the other as they passed us.

'Are you two going to leave that man lying there?' mother said.

'What man's that love?'

We looked up the lane to see the man struggling to his feet and staggering of further up the lane. Then the sound of a back gate's Suffix latch. The man was a neighbour. But who was he?

'Maybe we should start going in by the front door, mummy. I said. But, she wouldn't have any of that.

'It was better to see this than bring bad luck into the house,' she said.

Then something else happened on another Saturday evening that changed her mind entirely. We'd always come directly up the back lane coming home from the pictures. But now mother decided that we'd walk the full, twenty-five house length of St.Patrick's Terrace, passing our front door. Then enter our back lane from the top. Mother thought

31

that somehow this would lessen the chance of us seeing something nasty.

'We'll hear anything sooner, give us a chance to turn back,' said mother. But that chance didn't happen a few Saturday's later. On entering our lane, from the top, we heard the sound of scuffling, a woman moaning. Mother glanced at me.

'Well, she said,' it's not the police.'

No, she was right, it wasn't the police. The breeze stiffened in the lane. The full moon broke cover. And there as though in the blaze of sunlight, a man in a dark navy uniform, one hand clutching at a crazy little white hat on a head of dark hair, had a girl pinned up against the wall. The little white hat looked familiar.

She'd her legs wrapped round his waist. Her hands scissored at the back of his neck. He was thrusting into her as though he wanted to drive her through the wall. At every thrust the girl moaned. Three or four big cigarette butts lay on the ground, two still smouldering and flaring in the stiffening breeze.

'Jesus Mother of God, as if policemen, card players, 'pitch, and tossers' weren't enough,' mother said. Our back lane has gone to hell. It's become a dark den of iniquity.' She took my hand. 'Come on John, we're going back.'

'What's 'iniquity' mean mummy?'

The sailor turned his head to look at us. Spotting me, he took his hand of the little hat, which sailed to the ground, put his index finger up to his lips. He didn't stop thrusting. His eyes were glistening in the glare of the full moon. I knew then where I'd seen that crazy little white hat before and the head it was on, the eyebrows marching across the forehead in an undulating wave.

The stiffing breeze caressed the smouldering cigarette butts. They flared in the dark as the full moon took cover in the thickening clouds.

'I know...' I said.

'Never mind John, let's get home.'

It was the same American sailor who used to school my brothers and me on how to play baseball (we called it rounders'). The 'bases' for this game were the concrete squares used to anchor the barrage balloons designed to ensnare German warplanes during the Second World War. Although these barrage balloons, a hop and skip from Messines Park, didn't stop German bombers from blowing up houses there.

These schooling games of 'rounders' took place in a big empty field opposite St. Bridget's Avenue. The avenue on the other side of our back lane. The side our sailor boy had the girl up against.

'A Dixie cup hat', he'd said, when I asked him the name of the little crazy hat that never left his head. Until that night. And he'd asked me if I'd any sisters. 'No end of them,' I'd told him.

From that night, mother and I used the front door when coming in home from the pictures. It was what I'd heard another American sailor boy say, 'a tough call', for mother. But, she still wouldn't go *out* the front door.

And I'd to swear to her, on penalty of being feed cotton wool sandwiches for the rest of my life, that I'd not tell the others we'd started using the front door.

Or the reason. Riveting an all as that reason was to an impressionable young and innocent boy.

On the Sunday morning, following the American sailor's 'den of iniquity' incident, the sound of card and pitch and toss players drew me to the back lane again, like fillings to a magnet. I came out our back gate. Walked the short distance to the bottom of our lane. Traipsed the full front length of our terrace and entered the lane from the top as mother and I had done the previous night.

A card school was in full swing. I walked past. Stopped, came back to where mother and I had stumbled on the girl and the sailor. The cigarette butts were gone. But smoke rose from two or three of the card players.

The strong smell of the tobacco told me they weren't smoking weak, thin 'Woodbine'. But 'heavy duty' American 'Camel' or 'Chesterfield'. One of the men had a little white hat on, set off at an angle.

'Would you look at this', said one of the card players. 'Bloody Yanks.' He'd a clear crinkly tube with what looked like spits of gob at the bottom, held up for all to see.

'What's that?' I said.

He looked round. 'Hello little boy,' he said. (I didn't like this 'little boy' bit) Then, laughing, ' you run along home to your mummy now, little boy.'

Another piped up, blowing smoke down hairy nostrils, 'if your daddy had had one them little beauties you'd not be here now.' All the card players burst out laughing.

What was all that suppose to mean?

I didn't know then, that what I later knew as 'French letters', would have taken mother out of the tyranny of biology, but whose consensual use would have condemned her immortal soul to the eternal fires of a catholic hell. And would have presented mother with another 'tough call'.

And I didn't know then, what I later knew, that it wasn't just the breeze that had stiffened in our back lane that Saturday night. And the sailor boy clutching at his 'Dixie cup hat' brought with it a whole new meaning to the phrase, 'hold on to your hat'.'

Card and pitch-and-toss players preferred a Sunday. Policemen and their informers settled on Saturday. And Saturday night was also the choice for clandestine liaisons with American sailors by local girls. But other events broke out in midweek in our back lane that mother thought of as a general hive of 'iniquity'.

One Wednesday, sitting quietly with mother peeling potatoes in our scullery, there erupted, in the stillness of the afternoon, a high-pitched girl-like screaming. Mother and I looked at one another. Then more screaming and wailing.

We rushed out, there to see it already full of our neighbours on both sides of the lane. They were standing silently at their back gates with their arms folded across their bosoms. Each one looking, occasionally, at the other.

A black, shiny car had reversed up our lane. It stood engine idling, a few doors down from our neighbours, the Smiths. They lived opposite, but two doors further down. They'd been small pig farmers in County Derry. Big horse-faced jowly women and men.

You could imagine these men standing at the side of their piggeries having slow deliberate, ruminative discussions about pigs and crops and who's buried in which section of the cemetery and when it'd be their turn, the price of grass seed...

Through the back window of the car we saw a priest at the wheel. A Nun sat next to him Two other priests, each with an arm of the struggling and wailing Smith were dragging him towards the car.

The Nun turned around to see what was happening. She'd a long white scar across her top lip. I recognised her. She and another Nun had called at our front door on a collection mission. They were both from the 'Sisters of Nazareth' in Bishop Street.

His hair, always immaculately groomed, according to mother, now an unkempt mess. Mascara running down his cheeks. He was 'effing and blinding' good style in a high-pitched voice.

He wrenched one of his arms free of the big priest. With

35

his index finger he smeared his bright red lipstick across his mouth, his heavy purple eye shadow he dragged onto his forehead. Bundled now into the back of this black shiny car, to be taken away and 'cured' under the tender mercies of the 'Sisters of Nazareth.' His name was Alan Smith. (He preferred Alison) He was thirteen years of age when they came for him.

Under mother's watchful eye we all carried out our household chores. My sisters would make the beds with the usual 'blankets'. Help mother with the dishes, preparing food in the little scullery... We boys sweep clean the back yard, tidied the front garden, put the sloop bucket out for the pig man. This, generally, without a murmur or a word of protest. And on completion of these household chores, once in bed, we all soon fell asleep. Suitably tired out.

But on the night of our aunt's visit there was no sleep in any of us children. Chores or no chores.

Every Saturday before the visit, mother gathered us all together in the kitchen. She told us that we were never, ever, to let anyone know that she used overcoats for blankets. And especially not our aunt. Banished to a toffee-less desert Island we'd all be if we did. She said this with such grim earnestness that we all of us believed her. Every Saturday morning mother changed the present overcoats for different recently washed ones.

Mother told us just to think of these overcoats as blankets with arms. She was mortified that she couldn't afford proper blankets. And ever more mortified that she had to use overcoats in place of proper blankets.

Another source of mortification for mother was the pushing and shoving and noise of all us children as we fought to get to the front of the queue for the toffees. This the polar opposite to how we pushed and shoved each other to get to the *back* of the queue for the dreaded Senna Pods.'

'Now, now, our aunt would intone, in her la- di- da voice. Stop that.' And she'd immediately stop handing out the toffees, screwing up her face in disgust. 'Mary, for goodness sake, can you not control these children of yours.' You need to get a bit of 'rick' on them.'

She sounded as though she'd some of the plums she'd brought for mother and father in her mouth. That is until she used the word 'rick'. Here the Northern Irish accent kicked in good style.

Mother mortified by our behaviour, made it a rule that from then on, three of the girls, or we three boys were in our respective bedrooms before our aunt called.

It was the following morning before *they* saw any toffees. With three of we children, sometimes four, in bed before her visit, it meant that our childless aunt wasn't overwhelmed by a human wave of jostling children, not one of whom had seen a toffee since the previous Saturday or Sunday.

Those whose turn it was to be in bed when our aunt called, and didn't get their toffees until Sunday, would endlessly tease the others who'd eaten theirs the night before.

Even so, those whose turn it was to go to bed before our aunt came were never happy about it. And tantrums and outright rebellion shimmered and shone on grimaced faces as they were escorted to early bed by a determined mother.

One Saturday evening when three of my sisters, Gerty, Ann and Eleanor, whose turn it was, were in bed and just as our aunt was handing out the toffees, an almighty ruckus broke out upstairs.

Mother apologising to our aunt, pulled open the sitting room door, flew up the stairs in a frantic flurry of arms and legs. She was out to quell the rebellion of those mutineers whose turn it was to go to bed, but who thought otherwise. Silence reigned upstairs three seconds after she'd left our aunt's presence.

When she came back down the stairs she left the sitting room door open for an even swifter flight, should the need arise. She apologised again to our aunt.

It was during this awkward silence, between, when our aunt had finished handing out the toffees and after mother made her frantic flight upstairs to quell the mutineers and her arriving back in our kitchen that the shrill voice of Gerty sounded in loud and vengeful protest.

'Mummy', she roared, (with the lungs of ten children) Ann's pulling the arms out of the blankets. 'With the sitting room door wide open there was no escape from this devastating indictment. I'll never forget the look on my poor mother's face. She was mortified beyond redemption.

She bowed and buried her head in both hands. I'd not seen mother like this before. Nor had any of us. We crowded around her. Even or aunt was moved to come and put her hand on mother's shoulder. 'It's all right Mary', she said.

I noticed the liver spots on her hands. And her face looked older, almost haggard. Funny how'd I'd not noticed these things on our aunt before. Too pre-occupied with what she brought down with her on a Saturday for we children I suppose.

Father, who'd been scratching around on his bench in the scullery, came in and took mother in his arms. This was new territory for everyone. None of us had ever seen father show such public emotion and tenderness toward mother. 'Don't cry Mary', he said. He glanced at our aunt who'd now sat down, her hands crossed on her lap.

Mother turned to her.' Why, all of a sudden, after all these years, did you decide to come down here?'

Our aunt was silent. Then she said, 'You know I worked for the McDivvits for years. I was part of the family there. They shared everything with me. She stopped here at looked at father. 'And I thought your John would be re-assured by my presence.

Father gave her a brief nod of his head.

What was all that supposed to mean?

But 'Mary' had had enough. Now on a Saturday evenings mother and I went to the pictures. I never saw my aunt Gertrude again until the day of my first communion. At that time, she sent word down to father with one of aunt Annie's bricklaying sons Billy that she wanted to see me.

Gambling Man

The parish priest of Saint Patrick's chapel in Pennyburn, (we never said Church) Father Glackin, called it, not Pennyburn, but 'Half-Pennyburn' because of how little the Sunday collection amounted to.

He should be so lucky! Grown men had better things to do with what little spare coins they had, hence the card, pitch and toss schools in the back lanes.

On Sunday our back lane was, strictly speaking, off limits to me by an interdict of mother's. She disapproved of card, and pitch and toss schools there. 'Along its heathen length' as she had put it. But our back lane wasn't the only back lane in Pennyburn

In another one, behind St. Francis's terrace, and just across from Kelly's field stand the saints robed in their stained glassed windows on the chapel's side. The watery sun, glinting weakly on their frowning, leaden brows. A frowning I saw replicated through our kitchen window from the overhanging eaves of the houses of St. Bridget's Avenue on the other side of our back lane. This frowning always made my head dizzy. But I just shook the dizziness away.

Here in this dirt lane, well away from my own, I watched men dressed in their Sunday best, some playing cards others 'pitch and toss'. The card players' squat. The pitch and toss merchants upright in a tight bunch. All eyes following the tossed pennies as they tumble back to the dirt lane. The pitcher the winner of all those coins that land 'heads up'.

There's usually about five schools of cards going on at any one time. I prefer watching those. I drift between them watching the action.

I stop at the third school. I know two of the men. Jimmie Coyle, a cabinetmaker, who works alongside father. And Fred McLaughlin, who thinks he's going out with my sister Bridy. I get a curt nod of recognition from both as I sidle up to the game.

These men are crouched down on their hunkers. A pool of pennies their heads and tails, dingy and faded, lie glumly in the middle. The entrance fee, the 'pot', to the game of three-card brag.

The dealer shuffles the pack, bright yellow, with a blue and white trim, a greyhound in the middle, its finely shaped, delicate head out of kilter on a deck of cards. A new pack as always on a Sunday, crisp and clean, and as fresh as a newly minted coin. This new pack of cards, hammered with use through the week. I only watched on a Sunday.

'Anyone want to cut?' the dealer says, offering the pack around. A man leans across, lifts half the pack, and places it under the other half. The dealer, his chin on his chest, gives each player an up-from-under look. He flicks the cards at speed around the crouching men.

I love the sweet, innocent sound of the individual card as it's flicked from the deck, the sound of a raw carrot being broken in two. A gust of wind blows through the back lane. Three down-facing cards for each man. The wind's attempt to turn the cards wrong way up is stifled by the hunkered circle of serious-faced men.

'It's down to you,' says the dealer to the first man on his left who looks at his cards.

'I'll brag thrupence,' he says, throwing a three penny

piece into the pool as he stands up with the cards held into his chest. I watch his eyes as they swivels round each of the players gauging their reaction. Three pence is a lot of money here. He must have a brilliant hand.

Or he's bluffing. Some one of the other players will know from past form whether he is or not.

'Cost you three pence to see,' says the dealer. Or fourpence to up it.' Those whose hands are poor, or are frightened by the 'three penny' bet, dump their cards into the middle.

'I'll up it to fourpence,' says the last man, throwing a three penny bit and a penny into the pot.

'Fourpence to see, fivepence to up it,' says the dealer to the man who bet three pence.

I scan the stone-carved faces of these two players. I wait holding my breath waiting for the next move in the game. The chapel bell rings for the start of another Mass. The watery Sun moves on. The frowns on the leaden brows of the saints deepen as though in contemplative empathy with the two players. The wind stiffens in the lane.

'I'll see,' says the man who bet the three pence.

Years later, as an apprentice shop joiner, when asked by the shop foreman, Eddie Hughes, to go to Edmondson's, the hardware store at the bottom of Shipquay Street and ask for a 'long stand' I 'd look at him, waiting for the next move in the game.

As I leave the back lane, heading home, I stand for a moment and watch a small group of four starting to play pitch and toss. From about three yards each tosses a penny at a small hole. A hole that we boys use as a point in marbles. The first in the hole gets to shoot first at the other player's marble. The nearest to the hole, not in it, in the game of pitch and toss gets to toss the pennies into the air.

These card games were unusually civilized affairs,

creating as they did a kind of solidarity among the players. Each player focused exclusively on the cards. But also part of a team. The first school of serious concentration I ever attended. Play started early. After the first mass at nine o'clock. I always went to early mass.

During the course of the morning players would come and go. Either going to Mass or coming back from it. The card game itself was to me, like the Mass, a communal, but secular event. All individuals sure, but the sense of this communal gathering reminded me of when we were children dancing and laughing around the tin bath in our back yard as our feet did the weekly wash. But quiet. More intense. But still that great sense of being caught up in something bigger that yourself.

A few with iron in their arteries saw the Sunday card playing as a desecration. And from time to time, they'd gather in the back lane and attempt to disrupt the playing. But just as in cards, where you need a certain strategy to win, there's a general rule, in pontoon for example, not to twist at thirteen, but sit tight, a more robust strategy was needed to deal with this iron-artery contingent.

I witnessed such a strategy one Sunday. Joe Ferry our milkman was an amateur boxer. He fought lightweight. A leftie. Small, wiry, intense, with a boxer's body heat that burnt on touch. Ankles you could cut cheese with. He threw a punch quicker than the wind from a duck's ass. But there was a vicious edge to his boxing, as I was to witness that Sunday and in later years, when he married my sister Ann.

The card players stopped playing and fell silent as this motley crew of three approached.

Just as they did when policemen came into the lane looking for someone. Although everyone knew there were police informers among them. Just not who.

'Do you not think that Jesus would weep, seeing you gambling on a Sunday,' said one. The other two nodded their heads in dumb unison. I recognised the one who spoke. Nigel McDermott, a big thickset man who liked a drink or two from the state of his bulbous purple stained nose. I recalled something about him having a go at becoming a priest. But he hadn't it in him. Still thought himself 'holier than thou' though.

All the card players knew Joe. And waited for him. Joe picked out McDermott. The biggest in the bunch. A good place to make an example.

McDermott is standing with his hands by his sides. Joe fires his right twice into McDermott's face. As he puts up his mitts to protect his face, Joe, leaning into him, steadies himself, plants his feet, socks McDermott twice with a left to the right side of the rib cage. A liver punch. McDermott's eyes, popping out of his head, his nose pouring blood is falling to the ground. Joe steps in close, low, and drive a left into his crouch. Neither of the other two move.

'Pick him up and get him out of here,' Joe said, turning his back on them. They picked him up and slink off down the lane. If they'd been dogs their tails would've been way between their legs. A low mummer ripples through the players as they nod to Joe. 'Right, said Joe, rubbing his bloodied knuckles with the palm of his hand, let's get back to it.'

Not for a moment, did even these card-player haters think of calling the police. Nobody calls the police here for anything. It was hard for me not to like Joe that morning. Although I grew to hate him after he'd married my sister Ann and beat her to the ground just as he'd done to McDermott that Sunday morning.

When I got a paper round delivering the 'Belfast Telegraph' around Pennyburn, including Messines Park every bit of money I earned went into playing cards on a Sunday in the back lane behind St. Francis Terrace.

By this time the pennies had morphed into shillings, half crowns. I especially loved the Irish half crown with the Irish Hunter horse and the Irish harp. The range of the card games now included five and seven card draw and the old favourite, three-card brag. Now I was a proud member of the Father Glackens's club of 'Half-Pennyburn.'

In the wintertime, the card schools re-located to one of the houses in St. Patricks Terrace, number twenty-nine. Raymond Sweeney lived there with his mother and brother. The brother had a throat problem. You could barely hear him when he spoke. I called him 'squeak'.

Sweeney's father died in the First World War. He fought alongside the Nationalist and Unionists from Messines Park at the Battle of Messines. Catholic and Protestant united in a common cause, albeit for different reasons.

You paid Sweeney an entrance fee, which he gave to his mother. She took up with the guy who owned the 'Collin Bar'. And later Raymond became the manager of that bar. 'Squeak' helped. Neither Sweeney ever played cards. A good card player, which I was, is like a good snooker player, the sign of an ill-spent youth.

Father Glackin

The public transport buses didn't come up the Buncrana Road to Pennyburn in the fifties. On Tuesday afternoons mother and I would sometimes go for a stroll.We'd walk past St. Patrick's chapel to the British Navy base, passing the Lough Swilly train and bus depot. We'd sometime call in and see uncle Fred, father's brother. He worked there as a mechanic.

As we passed St. Patrick's chapel mother pointed to the life-size statue of St. Patrick on the right hand side set back in his own alcove. Arms and head raised up to the heavens. Christ, his head in a wreath of thorns bowed down in death on his crucified cross, topped the bell tower. The cross cast its frowning shadow at me and over the chapel entrance.

I once had this horrible dream about a huge head made of transparent congealed rubber. I was cutting into this head with a large kitchen knife. As I cut into its thin streams of zigzag blood leaked through it, like red-forked lightning. I told my sister Maureen of this dream.

'You must have done something dreadful,' she said. 'No one has such a horrible dream for no reason. You are a very wicked little boy. What have you done?'

This frightened me more than the dream. I wondered if that was why the overhanging roof eaves of St. Bridget's Avenue, across the back lane, were always frowning at me just like Christ on his cross was now. Mind you Maureen had a knack of putting the wind up me.

One night when I was in front going up the stairs to bed, candle in hand (there was no gas-lamp on the stairs) there was an explosion of thunder.

I dropped the candle. It went out. I stood stock still, trembling. Forked lightning flashed, illuminating the stairs. Then another rumbling explosion of thunder. And another flash of lighting. To boot, Maureen, just behind me, grabbed my ankle. I screamed the house down, tripping over the candle, leaping up the staircase two treads at a time to the relative safety of our gas-lit bedroom.

Ann pushed Maureen out of the way and followed me up. She put her arms around me. 'It's only God moving the furniture about,' she said.

'What about the lighting Ann?' I said.

'That God looking for his son.' She turns to Maureen, ' I saw that.'

'Do you know why St. Patrick's got his out-flung arms and head raised up to heaven?' mother said.

I didn't.

She told me that during the war German planes attempted to bomb the British Navy base on the Strand Road. During the raid, one of the bombs went astray, heading for a direct hit on St. Patricks chapel. It was a Sunday morning. The chapel, as usual was packed. And as Father Glackin was taking Mass that day the card, pitch and toss contingent were at the back of the chapel as usual in readiness for a quick exit after communion.

St. Patrick's head, slumped down onto his chest, his arms by his side, up until that moment, flung both head and arms up to the heavens. The bomb, miraculously diverted, exploded in the sand pit directly across from the chapel.

After which St. Patrick's head again slumped onto his chest. His arms returning to his side, his poised and sedate serenity exuding calmness, and spiritual certitude. The parochial house sustained some superficial bomb damage. There were no casualties in the Chapel.

'Why are his arms outstretch, and his head raised now?' I said

Mother said the raid itself wasn't much of success (in so far as the Germans were concerned) as no ships were hit. But after the short raid, one of the German bombers, homeward bound, jettisoned a further bomb. This too was heading for a direct hit on the chapel. Again St. Patrick flung his arms and head up to the heavens. And the sand pit across the way took delivery of a second German bomb that day.

After the second bomb, miraculously diverted as the first bomb was, St. Patrick's, arms and head remained permanently flung up to the heavens in supplication and thanks.

His outstretched arms and raised head are today seen as his personal guarantee of the physical and spiritual safety of all within the chapel. And a reminder to us all of the power of saintly outstretched arms and raised head.

Clever old St. Patrick. Not content with driving snakes out of Ireland, he's now also fêted as the first and only catholic bomb disposal saint. This accolade granted to him for his disposing of German bombs into the heathen grounds of the sand pit. And away from the holy consecrated grounds of the chapel, where the congregation is now, and forever, safely and spiritually ensconced.

'Is that why we always make the sign of the cross when we pass the chapel, to thank Saint Patrick?' I said.

'That's as good a reason as any. But we cross ourselves because the body of Christ's in the chapel,' mother said. Going to early Mass with father on Sundays and with mother on 'holydays of obligation', I don't remember ever seeing Christ's body. But I reminded myself to be on a special look out the following Sunday.

I knew from a very early age, that it is a mortal sin not to go to Mass on Sunday. This is a guaranteed trigger for Mass attendance. If you die with a mortal sin staining your soul, you go straight to hell. Holy day of obligation carry the same stricture.

I worked, years later, on the new Catholic school, St. Mary's, in the Creggan Estate and I watched men slip away, during working hours to attend a holyday of obligation Mass in the Creggan chapel, it too called St Mary's. Many holy days of obligation fell during the working week.

The priests laid on early Masses. Too early for some. Even though these men knew they'd lose their jobs if caught, it made no difference. The loss of their jobs paled into insignificance when compared with the loss of their immortal souls to the eternal catholic fires of Hell, promised them should they miss Mass on a Sunday or a holy day of obligation.

The priest that father had a lot time for was Father McCauley. But even he had his moments. Father, who'd been off sick for a few days in October, one of which was a Thursday and a holy day of obligation, the feast of St. Francis of Assisi, went to the eleven o'clock Mass with me.

Younger men, who would not work, had into the habit of lying in after a heavy day playing cards and 'pitch and toss' in ours and others' back lanes. The younger women were busy having more babies, or working in the 'Tilly and Henderson' shirt factory. The majority of the congregation was retired and elderly people.

When Father McCauley mounted the pulpit even the card, pitch, and toss players stayed put. They knew his form. He's be all of five minutes in the pulpit. But this holy day of obligation turned out to be a little different.

'I'm going to address a complaint, by some, of our congregation,' he said. Everybody's ears picked up. The card and pitch and toss contingent looked at one another.

'The plank of wood you kneel down on, good honest pitch pine by all accounts, during Mass, is thought by some to be uncomfortable on their poor catholic knees.

Father Glackin may refer to 'Pennyburn' as 'Half Pennyburn' because of the amount of donations collected during Mass. And in that instance, I agree with him. This complaint by some, can only be fully answered by an increase in those donations for the Parish to afford something more amenable for those long suffering catholic knees.'

The card and pitch and toss continent grew restless, glancing over their shoulders at the exit. Father McCauley went on to blast those who'd complained.

'In catholic Ireland, even here in Northern Ireland, during 'Penal Times, ' the congregation was forced to say Mass in fields, barns, the open countryside. In rain, hail and snow. Which they knelt down in. Here in your chapel you have a solid, dry, honest piece of pitch pine wood to kneel on.'

I glanced behind me as the exit door slammed shut. The card and pitch and toss contingent were gone. And it seems to me, that it's only the good people of Pennyburn, or Half-Pennyburn, as Father Glackin says, who want to pray in comfort at no expense to themselves.'

On he goes on this subject for another solid fifteen minutes. Even father started to get restless. I was beginning to think that Father Glackin wasn't such a bad spud after all. At least you knew what to expect from him. And it was his turn to say the early Mass the following Sunday.

At that early Mass with father, the heavenly flung out arms and raised head of St. Patrick's appeared under a new less-saintly guise.

'Father Glackin', father said at Mass that Sunday, in a

voice strong and steady, as I'd never head it before. 'Father Glackin', he said again. The whispering in the chapel stopped. Heads turned to see who had called out the priest's name.

Father, who'd stepped out into the aisle, waited until he had the priest's full attention. 'You know, Father, you don't think than maybe Jesus Christ might be more pleased to hear the innocent crying of children's voices than you own.'

Father Glackin was silent. Then after a brief pause, although it felt like an hour to me, he said. 'Well spoken John Boyle.'

John Boyle, the priest had said his name, my name. And that was all he said. Then father was beside me again. My throat filled with something hard, my heart thudded like a boot in a washing machine. I touched father's coat cuff. He looked at me and smiled. I nearly told him I loved him then.

When Father Glackin took Sunday mass, the card and pitch-and-toss contingent, sat in the back pews, or stood behind them. And once holy communion was over they'd slip out before he mounted the pulpit. Once started, Father Glackin took some stopping. On this particular Sunday, he took some starting.

He had always relished the sound of his own voice, genuflecting his head up and down as though in adoration of himself as he spoke, raising his outstretched arms. But, there were other sounds in the chapel that Sunday he clearly didn't relish.

Just before Mass began that Sunday, father and I were seated in the central aisle, near, but not at, the back. 'I'm not sitting among them tossers,' father said when I suggested we sat right at the back because it was Father Glackin who was taken the Mass. Mass was a felt event for father. But even he got figitity when Father Glackin inhabited the pulpit.

Father like mother, had similar views of the card and pitch and toss contingent. I didn't tell either of them how much I enjoyed watching 'them 'tossers' at their cards and pitch, and toss schools. And I hoped that father used the word 'tossers' in its relation to those who played the game of 'pitch and toss', rather than its more risqué use.

The congregation was hushed with only a low rustling sound of voices issuing through the chapel like a light wind through fallen leaves. We children would fidget, yes. But, mothers' would quell their noisy, crying children with a sugar-laden dummy. And a barrage of 'Shsses'.'

During this Mass the murmuring largely ceased with only the hushed, almost inaudible sound of Father Glackins's voice, his back to us, intoning in Latin. It was only at times like the Introit, for example, that you could clearly hear his voice as he said, 'Dominus Vobiscum', and we answered, 'Et Cum Stpitu tuo'.' But during the elevation of the chalice, after the consecration the congregation fell completely silent and still, as though painted into their pews. |You could have heard the wafer-thin communion host fall.

Father knew the four priests of the Pennyburn parish better that most. He'd taken the 'pledge' and didn't drink alcohol. He carried the 'Pioneer's lapel pin with an image of the 'Sacred Heart' to discourage people from offering him drink. And the Fathers, in their divine wisdom, regularly called upon him to tend the bar at various money-raising priestly functions.

They knew he'd not be firing the drink into him at these regular functions, nor discreetly ferreting the odd bottle home. Father nicknamed Father Glackin, noted, among other things for his money raising talents, Father 'money bags.' But Father money bags had other less welcome traits

This particular Sunday Father Glackin was gathering himself together in the pulpit. The card and pitch and toss contingent had slipped away quietly as usual after communion. But this Sunday was different. It seemed the whole chapel was full of crying babies each one competing one with the other. And each one with a sound future as a prospective soprano opera singer.

His brow furrowed, jaws clinching Father Glackin waited a few moments for silence to fall giving the congregation as a whole, and the mothers' of the noisy children in particular, a series of his up from under looks.

Now his arms were by his side. His head slumped onto his chest looking down at his feet. Then his patience went AWOL. And just like Saint Patrick, he flung his arms and head heavenwards, appealing not only to the mothers' of the keening children, but to God himself.

It struck me that these gestures were as much to do with him trying to keep the short fuse of his temper at bay as they were about an appeal to God or mothers'.

'Would the mothers' of those children, either take them outside, or quiet them,' he said, dropping his arms by his side and allowing his head to sink onto his chest. In different parts of the chapel people rose in their pews allowing red-faced affronted mothers' to pass, lugging their wailing, innocent infants with them.

A murmur of disapproval hummed through the congregation. In different parts of the chapel men also rose from their pews and shuffled out with these mortified mothers. Father gently squeezed my arm and stepped out into the aisle.

All credit due then to St. Patrick for driving snakes out of Ireland and saving the chapel and those therein from the wrath of German bombers. No credit due to Father Glackin for driving the mothers' of wailing children out of the chapel. And all credit due to Father for his sober appraisal, and resolution to the brewing insurrection in the chapel that Sunday.

First Confession

The same Father Glackin heard my first confession. I entered the confession box and knelt down on the small raised wooden dais. I placed my arms as best I could on the shelf just below the little sliding door. This immediately shunted open to reveal Father Glackens's long horse-like frowning face.

When my Primary school master, Mr. Quinn, was schooling me what to expect and how to behave in the confession box, I told him I was afraid at the thought of having the priest staring at me as I confessed my sins.

'No priest looks at a penitent during confession, 'Mr. Quinn said.

'What's a penitent?'

He gives my head a curt slap with his thick-fingered hand.

'In aimn Anathar agus mhic agus a Spioraid naoimh', I began. I watched Father Glackens's brow furrow deepen, his jaw clinch.

'Is it going to be all Irish then?' he said.

'No, Father, I've only just started to learn it, but thought I'd get in a bit of practice.'

'Who teaches you the Irish?'

'Mr. Flanagan.'

'At school?'

'He can only teach it after school, Father.'

'Why's that you think?'

I told him I wasn't sure. The Father's breath smelt like a mixture of our cat's poo and stale alter wine.

'Bless me Father for I have sinned,' I intone as instructed. This is my first confession.'

'Go on my son.'

I told him I'd once tried to poison our cat.

'How'd you do that?'

I told him I'd found this evil smelling medicine bottle in the kitchen press and mixed it in with the cat's milk.

'What happen to the cat?'

I told the Father that it staggered round for a bit, passed a lot of smelly wind. I didn't want it to die in the kitchen. I let it out into our back lane. Here it fell to the ground and wretched its stomach up. If it died in the back lane, then no one would think I'd anything to do with it. Instead of dying it leaped up onto our back wall and strolled off. 'Nine lives' I thought. Or eight anyway.'

'Do you do that kind of thing often?'

I told him I just wanted to see what effect the medicine had on our cat. I don't think it was in my mind to kill the cat – at least not in our kitchen

'Go on my son.'

'I'm not sure if it's a sin Father but when I see people kissing and hugging and things I think that I want to do that too only I've no one to do it with.'

'Things,' he said. What things?'

I told him about the American sailor and the girl that mother and I'd seen in our back lane. And how mother was, for some reason, disgusted by this. And what one of the card playing contingent had held up, making a foul remark about 'Yanks?'

55

'As she should be', he said. Did what you see lead you on to impure acts?'

'Impure act Father?'

'Never mind,' he said. You'll know soon enough.'

I thought then that maybe what the Father meant by an 'impure act' was what I got up to on the rope swings on a tall sycamore tree in the plantation just beyond Saint Bridget's Avenue. There were two single ropes hung from parallel branches. I'd get this girl I knew to swing into me and me into her. I liked it when we bumped into one another. I don't know how she felt.

But she didn't seem to mind and after a while of this bumping into one another, thought it great fun. And fun wasn't exactly top of the agenda at Primary school. Or anywhere else. And especially when I was being briefed by Mr. Quinn on how to behave, what to do and what not to do during my first confession. Or anytime when in the presence of a priest, or him or so and so...

'Be respectful, Mr. Quinn had said. And contrite – don't you even think of asking me what contrite means Boyle,' he said before I could open my mouth.

I asked the Father if bumping into the girl in this way was an impure act.

'What were you thinking when you bumped into this girl?'

'I wasn't thinking of anything Father. I just liked doing it. It made me feel good. It wasn't like bumping into the tree. And the girl seemed to like it as well.'

'Hmm, he said.

'And does your mother tie a knotted binder at your back when you go to bed at night?'

'Why'd she do that Father?'

'To keep you from turning onto your back in the night.'

What was I supposed to make of that, turning on my

56

back at night?

'Do you say your prayers before you climb into bed?' Father Glackin said.

I told him I always made an act of 'perfect contrition' asking God to forgive me my sins every night. At Primary school we'd been taught that if you make an act of perfect contrition before you went to bed each night, you'd go straight to heaven should you have, the apparent, misfortune to die in the night.

'I sometimes wish Father I'd die in the night so I'd go straight to heaven,' I said.

'That's more like it,' he said.

'Can I ask you something Father?'

'Go on my son.'

'I can make an act of perfect contrition every night and God forgives my sins. Why do I have to come here Father?'

'What's your name?'

I told him.

'Hmm, he said. 'Did your master, Mr. Quinn, speak with you about how you're expected to behave during your first confession, or any confession?'

'Yes, he did,' I said.

I told him about the old tall fat man who lived in St. Patrick's Terrace. He had the first small black and white TV in the whole of Pennyburn, if not in the whole of Ireland. The snowy picture was forever jumping up and down the screen.

There were four of us boys who used to go up twice a week to see this T.V. He also had a set of Scottish bagpipes, including the drones. He'd remove the drones and play the pipes for us. I loved the sound of those pipes. A harsh, uncompromising, warlike sound.

'I can see I've got your interest little boy,' the old fat man said to me as he rubbed my knee with his hairy hand, his other pushing through his thick grey wavy hair. He said I

57

was his favourite little boy.

He taught me to play scales on the pipes. The other boys only wanted to watch the T.V. After awhile he allowed me to take the full set of pipes home to show mother and father. When I played this full set, with the drones, Bernadette, my youngest sister ran screaming from the room. I dropped the bagpipes and burst into tears at the thought I'd frightened my little sister so much.

'Was that a sin for me to have frightened my little sister like that Father?'

'Say a 'Hail Mary' and an 'Our Father' for your penance my son. And say a decade of the Rosary for me,' Father Glackin said. And tell your father to call down and see me in the parochial house tomorrow night.'

Why would he want to see father? I was about to ask him when he said. 'You're just like your father, aren't you young Boyle?' You like living dangerously, like the mouse that took up residence in the cat's ear'.

'What does residence mean Father?'

He raised his hand and made the sign of the cross, as he intoned, 'In nomine Patris et Filii et Spiritus Sancti.' As I left the confession box I wondered if I should have also told the Father what happened to me on the road to Burnfoot, just before I'd made my first confession. And whether that was a sin on my part or someone else's.

Father was a big pipe smoker and I'd walk the length of the Buncrana Road and over the border into a shop at Burnfoot in the Republic to get pipe tobacco for him.

There it was a third of the price. A rock solid powerfully smelling two-inch cube of compressed tobacco, 'Walnut Plug'.

I would sniff it a dozen times on the way home. It made my head dizzy. Not 'pass out' dizzy. Nice dizzy. Like the dizzy I felt when I flung myself back in bed, the blood spinning around in my head.

The Buncrana road was quiet during the day. This day, on a bend in the road, and a few hundred yards from Coshquin, a small village about two miles from Burnfoot, a man stepped out in front of me from a copse of trees. Young, fat, tall, with thick black wavy hair.

'Hello little boy,' he said. He spoke these words very slowly and deliberately with a pronounced country accent. I remembered a trip to County Derry where father had farming friends. The men there spoke with such solemnity that you felt they were handing down a sentence of some kind. 'And... You ... Will... Be taken... From this court...To Be...Hanged by the neck...' When all they were really saying was, 'Will you go out and brings the cows in?'

Anyway, this fat man had uncovered himself. And his huge thingy was stuck out in front of him. I didn't think anything was wrong. He's a grown man. I trusted him. It's broad daylight. I remember the very sweet taste of the conical shaped pink sweet he gave me. And the little piece of white cream on the top of the pink sweet. But I don't remember anything else.

It was only later that a sense of unease entered me. And my mouth felt dry and wet at the same time just as it had done then. I knew that something not right had happened. I never told anyone. Because I didn't really know what had happened. I never went for pipe tobacco for father again. I felt as though somehow he'd in some vague way betrayed me.

First Communion

I'd always been in two minds about Messines Park The name itself was enough to confuse me. Messines Park? All of my little terraces and avenues in the enclave of 'The Collon', Pennyburn, had saints names. I related and responded to them without question. St. Patrick's Terrace, St. Bridget's Avenue, St. Francis's Terrace...'

But here now, in St. Patrick's chapel, were two boys from Messines Park being inducted along with four of us from the saintly terraces and avenues, by Father Glackin into what Holy Communion was all about. What we were to expect. And what he expected of us. The chapel was empty but for we boys. Father Glackin had just shot off saying, 'be back in jiffy boys, behave.'

I turned to the Messines Park boys. 'What are you two doing here?' We don't know you – do we?' I said to Jimmie McDaid, who sat next to me.

'I'm Nigel and this Edgar,' said the bigger of the two boys. And we're catholic just like you.'

'Nigel and Edgar?' Jimmie said. Where'd they get names like that but by living in Protestant Messines Park?'

'What's you last names?' I said.

'Nigel Sweeney and Edgar McBride.'

'There's no Catholics in Messines Park,' said Jimmie. They're all Prods.'

'You only say that because my Dad's a policeman,' said Nigel.

'A policeman?' I said. Would you for God's sake listen to this young fella, a policeman no less.'

'Ask Father Glackin when he gets back,' said Nigel. He'll tell you.'

.Little John McKeever pipes up, 'They're a bunch of Brits, that's what they are, all of them in Messines Park.'

Nigel lunged across and grabbed McKeever's shirt and twisted it into a white knot just as Father Glackin came barrelling back.

'What's going on here?' Unleash that boy's throat Sweeney.'

Nigel Sweeney. Can you believe that?

'OK Boyle, spit it out,' said Father Glackin.

'Just a bit of an argument about Messines Park,' I said.

'And?'

'That's all Father,' I said.

We went to the British Legion hut in the Collon lane, at the back of Messines Park, on a Saturday afternoon to watch black and white movies. Who else was I to think was in the 'British Legion' but Brits? And weren't all Brits Protestants? We used to go into Messines Park in the evenings to clip the heads of flowers in their gardens with our slingshots.

And there were a lot of the houses in Messines park with orchards full of apples, pears and green gauges. These we use to pinch, filling our belted pullover with them. We wouldn't have done that had they not been Brits, would we?

' For the record Boyle, these two boys' catholic fathers', whom I know, fought in the Great War,' said Father Glackin.

'You meant they were fighting for the Brits, Father,' I said.

61

'You've had your say Boyle,' Father Glackin continuing, 'there was this great battle at 'Messines' in Belgium....'

My Dad told me that where Messines Park gets its name,' said Nigel.

'... which is where, as Sweeney has just said, Messines Park gets its name.' And many Derry men fought there.'

'Why were they fighting for the Brits Father?' I said.

'They had their reasons. And you learning Irish during school and not after school was one of them.'

What was that supposed to mean? I knew a lot of people who lived in Messines Park weren't catholic because they bought the 'Belfast Telegraph', we catholic's, the 'Derry Journal. 'Why were they fighting for the Brits?' I said.

'Well, said Father Glackin, for one thing, they didn't want you to be taught Irish during school hours – or any hours.'

I asked if that was the only difference between catholic soldiers and Protestants soldiers who fought at the battle of Messines that one wanted to teach Irish during school and the other didn't.

'In a complicated nut shell Boyle, yes.' he said.

Father Glackin then went on to tell us that a German bomber had dropped a bomb on Messines Park in April 1941. Four ex-soldiers who'd fought at the battle of 'Messines' in the first world war were killed along with eight of their family members.

I told Father Glackin that my mother had told me that the German bomb was headed for a direct hit on St. Patrick's chapel during Mass, and that St. Patrick, whose head was bowed, his arms by his side at the time, had flung his head and his arms up to the sky and directed the bomb to the sand pit opposite where it exploded. And that this had happened twice. Which was why his head and arms were permanently flung up to the sky to prevent any further bombs hitting the chapel?

And that St. Patrick was now recognised by the catholic church as their first bomb disposal expert.

'You don't believe that shite, do you Boyle?' said McKeever, leaning over into me.

'Right Boyle,' that enough,' said Father Glackin.

Then: 'Still, there might well be some truth to that Boyle.' I've just told you the facts. But facts have nothing to do with faith or miracles. And Holy Communion is also a kind of miracle...' and on he goes.

A week later, I made my first communion.

My aunt Gertrude had got one of aunt Annie's bricklayer sons Billy, to get word to my father that she wanted to see me after my first communion. First things first was mother's response to this request.

There were twenty terrace houses in St. Patrick's Terrace. After I'd made my first communion I went round all of these twenty houses knocking on doors. They'd put some copper coins into the little tin tray mother had given me, pennies and halfpennies and farthings. 'Oh, doesn't he look lovely in that little suit and white shirt,' they'd say, bending down and tousling my hair. Then the same performance in St. Bridget's Avenue and St. Francis Terrace. It was exhausting work.

Opposite St. Patricks Terrace there was another terrace of houses that I knew not to knock on. That was where, mostly, Protestants lived.

One of them was a 'B' special. I watched him go out at night in his black uniform carrying a 'Lee-Enfield rifle with fixed bayonet. The brown crossed hatched handle of his .38 Webley revolver jutting out of the black leather holster pinned to his waist with a broad black leather belt.

After the talk from Father Glackin about Messines Park, I wondered if I should go round the houses there as well. But mother said no.

Pinned to the lapel of my suit was a cloth image, with serrated edges, of the 'Sacred Hear of Jesus'. A miniature edition of the big picture of the Sacred Heat of Jesus in our bedrooms. And two brown scapulars draped over my shoulders, one scapular to the back, the other to my front, and a white armband.

I never wore a pair of shoes before that you could see yourself in. I'd put them under the bed that night. And got up at least five times in the night to spit on them and polish the spit till the leather of the shoes shone as black as a beetle's back.

'Now, mother said, you can go and see your aunt, as she's requested.'

There was no knocker on aunt Gertrude's door. Only a huge letter-box. I rattled this. 'Come in John', she said. (what accent?) standing aside. She sounded like mother. The affected posh accent was gone.

She had a front room as well. But her's was different. Coloured wool covered the floor. It made no sound as I walked on it. A big sofa covered in dozens of little indentations and made of the same material as my shoes looked new.

Hanging down from the middle of the ceiling, on a white cord was a big round glass bowl inside of which was a pear-shaped glass. There was light coming from it. There was no smell of gas.

'My, she said, you do look smart.' Sit down. You're just how I remember your father when he was your age.' She's most definitely now talking like mother. I'd thought at first I was hearing things.

In the middle of the room a polished timber round table with four green upholstered chairs sat on a large mat full of colours with tasselled sides and edges. A large flowered-patterned dish of white powdery plums sat in the middle of the table. Placed around this dish were small transparent bags full of toffees. I counted ten bags.

A wireless on a built-in shelf at the side of the tiled fireplace, where a coal fire blazed and hissed, played a kind of music I'd not heard before. It wasn't loud. The way it rose and swelled reminded me of the slow green swell of the sea against the wall in Buncrana where we went in the summer.

'You still go to the pictures with your Mother?'

'Yes.

'Do you like that?'

'Yes.

'Is it still only on a Wednesday night you go?'

'Yes.

She took a plum from the dish and handed it to me. I put it in my pocket. The blankets with the arms thing was when I'd last seen her. Her eyes were now red-rimmed, her hands more mottled and thin. The flesh hung loosely under her chin. She'd a crossed-hatched brow and two deep creases each side of her scythe -like nose. Her face had a deep frown even when she smiled.

My sisters and brothers didn't mind mother and I going to the pictures on Wednesday nights. They got my share of the toffees. And our aunt, told father that it was alright that my brothers and sisters all stayed up on a Wednesday night on account of mother and me not being there.

What was the big house you worked in like?' I said.

She looked at me with her frowning and now surprised face. 'How'd you know about that?' Did your Father tell you?'

'Mother.

My aunt took me on a tour of the big house. The huge rooms with high ceilings. The bookcases in the main room filled with books. Blinds pushed up the windows were so high.

'What kinds of books?'

'All kinds, they were big readers the McDivvits.' I don't ever remember seeing the daughter reading though.'

'Would you take me there sometime aunty, so I can see the books?'

She gives me sideways glance, the makings of a smile puckering her mouth at the word 'aunty'.

'Is that what you always called me?' she said.

She told me that she cycled down to the McDivvits every day. They never left the house now. Aunt carried down some daily groceries. The road to the house, like the house itself had fallen into disrepair.

'Would you like some tea, John', she said. I heard the 'whoosh' of a gas cooker. But only a faint smell of gas. She poured the water into a delf teapot and wrapped a tea cosy around it.

'Would you like a biscuit John?' she said.

We didn't have 'biscuits' at home because I'd never heard the word 'biscuit' before. And when I put the first biscuit in my mouth a waterfall of saliva rushed over it. No need of dipping biscuits in tea here. At least not for me, as I watched my aunt dip her's sedately into the tea.

The music swelled and then abated and swelled again. It made me feel as though I was swelling with it. I could see she was listening to. Then a sweet sound. An individual cut-glass sound. 'What's that playing?' I said.

'A piccolo.

I remember the harsh screeching sound of the 'T' hinges on our ledged, braced and sheeted back gate, and the ensuing sweet sound after father had squeezed 'three in one' oil onto those grating ear-offending sounds. Chalk screeching across a blackboard.

'Piccolo', Piccolo, even the word sounds like music,' I said.

Her red-rimmed eyes were rheumy. I looked at her, reached out and touched her hand. She smiled, reached across and tousled my hair. 'You're a good boy,' she said.

'What were the McDivvits like to work for?'

She looked at me. 'They were demanding, but fair, in their own way. Always polite. Well spoken.'

'Did they teach you to speak like them aunty?' I said.

'I deserve that,' she said. Yes, they did. But that wasn't right. They taught me other things as well. Like listening to the music you're listening to now.'

'I like listening to that music,' I said. It's... different.'

She smiled a little. 'There's only the daughter left now. I stayed on to help her for a while after her mother and father died. But the big house was going to 'wrack and ruin. It wasn't her fault thought, the daughter's I mean,' said aunty.

'What's 'wrack and ruin mean?' I said.

Two hours had gone by. But it didn't feel like it. Now that I was on my own with my aunt I saw her in a different light. She seemed more intense, knowledgeable, old.

'I missed you both, when you weren't there on a Wednesday night you, and your mother,' she said, her head rising as the music rose. 'I'd no right to talk to your mother, telling her she needed to get this and that done.'

'I heard you tell mother once to get our range taken out,' I said. I didn't like that. I always put my chestnuts in the range oven to harden them for conkers at school.'

She smiled at this, reached across and touched my shoulder.

'I knew your mother was mortified that last Wednesday night I saw you both. But I never knew why.'

'Mother would gather us all together, just before you came on Wednesday night. She'd tell us all we must never let it be known to our posh aunt...'

'... is that what you called me?'

67

'... that we used coats for blankets.' And if we did, we'd be cast away to a toffee-less desert Island.'

At this she shook with laughter. 'Now, that's funny. A toffeeless-desert Island.'

'And I said, 'my sisters had let that particular cat out of the bag the last Wednesday night she was there by shouting down the stairs...'

'Yes, I remember, she said.' I just thought your mother wouldn't feel mortified by that. How stupid and inept I was to think that.' Her frowning face pulled into a creased grimace.

My aunt wasn't posh anymore. I laughed with her. Both at the fact she didn't know why mother had been mortified that night, and that she found it funny what mother said about a toffeeless desert Island.'

'Why aren't you talking the way you talked when you came down on Wednesday nights?' I said.

Her whole face creased again, like wind over water. 'I'd lost my way a bit.' I was left a bit of money by the McDivvits... It was just a silly, wicked pretence. But I care deeply for your father and thought my visits would, somehow, make him feel better.'

I understood what she meant by that last bit about caring deeply for father. But not about making him feel better. But I let it go. We listened to the music.

And after a while she said. 'I won't be coming down any more on a Wednesday night. Last Wednesday was the final time.'

'Why?'

She eased her arms out in front of her, palms upwards, head upright. 'It's just the way it is,' she said. Your mother'll be wondering where you are?' She leaned across the table, tousled my hair, stroked my cheek with her mottled, shaky hand. This was a different aunty entirely.

'Have you ever been to Boom Hall?' she said.

'No, but I know it's off the Culmore Road.'

She told me that in the surrounding grounds at the back of the great house there were a huge number of tall chestnut trees. And that these chestnuts weren't like the ones you usually see with their spiky green shell. These chestnuts were like big pears. They didn't have spiky green shells, but were smooth, just like a pear.

She gives me direction how to get there. Follow the river Foyle starting at the air raid shelters. It's an hour's walk. You'll find an avenue of trees starting behind the Boom Hall boundary wall. There you'll find your chestnuts at the end of this avenue of trees.

'Wouldn't it be better if I went the way you used to go?' I said.

'I don't want you to go that way'. It leads straight to the house. You don't want to go near the house.'

'Why, aunty?'

'Because I've asked you not to John,' she said. I want you to promise me you won't go near the house.'

'OK aunty, I said.

'Now you better go.' she said. She put the toffees into a large brown bag and the plums in another. 'You tell your mother, I'm sorry for my being the cause of her being mortified that Wednesday.' She handed me the brown bags.' Give her the plums and toffees. She can share them out between you. And tell her how I laughed at her casting you all away on a toffeeless desert Island. Not that your mother would ever do such a thing.' That was the third time I'd heard my aunt laugh.

As I left, the piccolo brought that sweet sound to my dull cloth ears. I walked ahead of her to the front door. I turned and she dropped to her knees and looked into my eyes. She put her arms around me and held me for a few seconds. I felt the woolly hair on her face caress my face. 'You tell your mother I'm sorry,' she said

I lifted my hand and put it on her shoulder. As she opened the door, she pressed two small disks into my hand. The door closed quietly behind me. I looked at what she'd pressed into my hand. Two Irish half crowns.

I told mother what my aunt has said. And told her about the music on the radio. 'I didn't know you could have a gas radio,' I said.

She gives me one of her wry smile. 'You can't,' she said. It's run on electric. Your aunt doesn't have gas lights, only a gas cooker. They're doing away with gas for lighting for our house as well. We're all going electric.'

'Electric'? That's why there'd been no smell of gas from the big bowl with the pear-shaped glass.

My aunt never did come again on Wednesday night to our house. But every Wednesday afternoon Brewster's bread van called with two large brown bags of plums and another large brown bag with ten transparent bags of toffees.

I only learned of my aunt's death, when, much later, one of aunt Annie's bricklayer sons came down and told father. Even after her death, the plums and the toffees came every Wednesday in Brewster's bread van.

School

I remember that first school morning as though yesterday. I was lying fast asleep when father shook my shoulder and beckoned me down stairs. He'd always been gone to work when I came down stairs in the morning.

We sat and I had a boiled egg and two slices of toast which he'd prepared. The coal fire in the range threw undulating shadows and warmth around the kitchen. He told me exactly where the house was he was working in. He'd scouted where it was best for me to come to him from the Rosemount school to have my soda-bread lunch with him.

'Come through the mesh gates leading into your playground and out the other mesh gates leading out of the playground. I'll be waiting there for you, this first time.'

He rose from the table and made ready for work. 'You wait now for your sisters John.' They'll be down in a minute and take you to school. I start work a lot earlier than you start school.'

This was the first time I'd heard father put so many words together consecutively.

'How far's it?' I said to mother after she and my sister came to the breakfast table.

Given the equivocal answer of, 'No further than everyone else goes,' put me on the alert. I didn't like these kinds of words. There was something borderline evasive about them. Even when they came from mother.

'Who's taking me?'

'As your father told you, you're with your sisters,' mother said.

'Aren't you taking me?' We go to the pictures together.'

'No. It's too far for me to go and come back each day.' I can't afford the bus fares for everyone and myself as well.' Impeccable logic from mother as usual.

Then to drive home this impeccable logic she said, 'In any case, as you know, your father's working on Marlborough Road. It's just across from the school. It's all arranged for you to go and see him and eat your scone bread there at lunch time.'

'Will you be there too?' I said.

In 1949, when I was six I started at Rosemount Primary school. I'd watched my sisters going to school. And knew it would be my turn sooner or later. It wasn't something I was looking forward to, this leaving mother.

My sisters all attended the 'Wee Nuns' in Francis Street. Rosemount Primary school was only a ten-minute walk away up through Brooke Park.

'Are all of my sisters taking me to school?' I said to mother.

'Ann knows where your school is.' The rest of your sisters need to know too.' mother said. She was never short of an answer. I looked forward to the day when I could ask her something that she couldn't answer.

Scrubbed up we set off for the bus stop at the bottom of the Buncrana Road. We passed Saint Patrick's chapel. We crossed ourselves. 'Do you know why Saint Patrick's arms and head are raised to heaven?' I said. 'It's because...'

'We know,' all three chorused.

We got off at the bus depot opposite Great James's Street. Ann took my hand as we all crossed the road. We went through Brooke Park, into the Lone Moor Road, from here into Helen Street and there was the Rosemount Primary school.

Long, wide tapering concrete steps lead up to the double front doors, huge, heavy brass handles glinting in the weak sunshine. My mouth was dry A sudden squall of rain hammered the steps as the sun hid behind a cloud. The wind tugged at my hair.

Boys shoaled past shouting and whistling at my sisters. This shoaling morphed into an orderly and quiet accent of the steps. Standing at the top of these steps was two men. One in a grey suit, tall burly. His big black shoes shone like wet coal. He took off his heavy horned-rimmed glasses and watched as my sisters and I approached. We all stopped at the bottom of the steps.

The other man, in a black suit, black tie, white shirt, black fedora hat, Father Glackin. Two other boys, whom I knew, Fred and Frankie McDaid, stood beside him in their scrubbed silence. Father Glackin beckoned us with his bent index finger. We all climbed the concrete steps. Ann told Father Glackin who we were.

'I know who you are. I know your father. You run along now girls to your own school. The wee Nuns will be waiting for you... who's picking John up after school?'

My sisters huddled into a little tight circle, like the pitch and toss players in our back lane. Only they weren't looking up waiting for coins to fall from the sky. 'I don't see why all of us should have come in the first place,' said Maureen. Typical comment for her.

'He's big enough to walk from our school on his own,' said Anglia.

It was Ann, who finally said, 'I will. I'd hoped it'd be Ann. And years later it was still Ann.

It was she, looking like Elizabeth Taylor, who took me

to my first dance at the 'Ritz' on the Strand Road. Spotted-faced as I was then, she proudly let the girls she worked with at 'Tilly and Henderson' shirt factory, at our end of the Craigavon Bridge, know that I was her brother. And that it was OK for them to dance with me. 'This's my wee brother.' Isn't he good looking? Just look at those eyes!' Ann would say.

I don't remember if any did dance with me, but, I never forgot Ann for this. Of all my sisters, she was the one I got on with the most. Not to say I didn't get on with the rest of them. After all it was a novelty for them to finally have a brother. No more that it was a novelty for me to have all these sisters.

Turning to me Father Glackin said, 'This is Mr. Duffy, your Head Master, and these other two boys... well I'm sure you know who they are.'

I knew who they were. How long had they been here? Mr. Duffy stuck his fat fingered hand out. I grasped it, my little hand lost in his.

'Your two friends have been here a few weeks,' said Father Glackin. You're the only boy from Pennyburn starting today. So in honour of your father, and you, I've asked Mr. Duffy's permission – he turned here and bowed slightly to Mr. Duffy, who curtly nodded his big bespectacled head – to bring the two wee McDaid's out to greet you along with my good self'.'

'Good self'"?

As I listened to Father Glackin, I wondered if he'd said Mass before he came here. He always talked funny after he'd said Mass. He was talking funny now. No doubt the altar wine got a sore touch before he arrived here. Mr. Duffy, who'd now put his glasses back on, looked over them, eyebrows raised at Father Glackin. He said nothing, stifling a yawn.

I was marched down a long corridor, class rooms either side. The two McDaids' ambled behind. Only the heads and shoulders of the boys in the classrooms were visible through the half-glazed doors. They sat upright and still at individual desks looking straight ahead.

The corridor's ceramic red floor tiles echoed under my feet. The kind of tiles you'd most likely find in a prison, or an Insane Asylum, like the one on the Strand Road before it became a Police station. The chalky odour in the corridor had a strong flavour of the flour mother used for baking.

At the last classroom door on the left, the headmaster stopped. He turned to us. 'Wait, he said as he entered. We three watched as he talked to the teacher. There was one empty desk at the back of the class. Mr. Duffy ushered us in.

'You two McDaid's, into your usual desks,' he said. Their two desks were at the front of the class. Mr. Duffy pointed to the desk at the back of the class as he looked at me. 'Sit I sat. Then, 'Stand. I stood. Call your name out to Mr. Quinn.' I call my name out. He wrote it down in a big roll book.

My desktop like all the others, had a fluted top for pens and pencils, a white ceramic ink well lipped over its cavity. The ink, bluey black, smelt like our cat's poo. Underneath the desktop, a full-length drawer.

Quinn's face was all nose. Thin, spidery reddish veins spread down this bulbous nose to his flared nostrils. I wondered if he'd started out being a priest before he became a music teacher.

As I was to find out, Quinn's nose was not his only disfiguring feature. In full view of the class, he'd gob into his handkerchief. Study this gob as though it might reveal some yet unknown, profound, but benign character trait of his. Then he'd look up at us and say, 'Well?

On an equally regular basis he'd tell the class that in trying to teach them a simple major scale, DOH, Re, Mi, Fa, Sol, La, Ti, DOH, on the recorder, he was 'wasting his sweetness on the desert air'. Very poetic. Unlike his constant gobbing into his hanky.

There were twenty-eight boys in the class and eight recorders. These were passed around from boy to boy. Each boy using an elongated brush on a wire handle to clean out his saliva before passing it on. Very hygienic. Quinn had his own recorder. He never passed it around.

Listening to the scale playing of most of the boys I could see why Quinn said he was wasting his sweetness on the desert air.

'Do you know the name of this instrument Boyle?' he said when my turn came.

'A chanter,' I said.

'A chanter?

I told him I'd played bag pipes and practiced at home on a 'chanter'. Which was pretty much what I was looking at now.

'Can you play a scale?'

'Do, Re, Mi, Fa, Sol, La, Ti, DOH.' I played with little breathless pauses between each note. I hadn't played the chanter for a while. And had never played a recorder.

'Well done Boyle,' Quinn said.

The big exception to scale playing on the recorder were the two McDaids. Their scale playing was effortless. My 'chanter' playing of scales were not as good as the McDaids' but good enough for Quinn to say, 'Well done Boyle.'

It was only later that I found out that he give extra lesson to the McDaids' as a standing favour to their father Jimmie.

At twelve noon the Angelus bell rang. 'Up, said Quinn. The whole class stood and recited the Hail Mary. 'Hail Mary full of grace the Lord is with thee, blessed art thou...'

A green-painted corrugated iron roof covered the outside lavatories. Just like the roof of our backyard coal shed. The urinals were two feet taller than me. Two meshed gates lead to where we played at lunchtime. It was just beyond these that I was to meet with father for lunch. He was second-fix joinering in a new housing estate in the Marlborough Road area, just across from the Rosemount School as mother had told me. Brian Friel, later to be my teacher at the new Saint Patrick's Primary school in Pennyburn, lived here.

On entering a house father was working in once, I heard music.

Music from a little portable radio.' John McCormick', he said when I asked him who it was singing. He watched me as I listened, listening as I was as when I heard the music on my aunt's radio.

Father told me he'd done a 'foreigner' for a friend of his, Jimmie McDaid, who lived in St. Francis Terrace, just round the corner from us.

'He's a teetotaller like me,' father said. He's in charge of the St. Columb's Brass and Reed Band. His two sons play in it.'

He said that Jimmie delivered fresh fruit to the American Base at Springtown Camp. He'd got friendly with this 'Yank'. He gave Jimmie the portable radio as a present as he was going back to the States. Jimmie gave father the radio as payment for building fixed-in cupboards for him at his home. The 'foreigner' in question

As well as music, father had a little primus stove where he brewed his tea. The sound of the music and the homely smell of his brewed tea I always remember. He waited for me before he lit the little primus stove. I loved the 'whoosh' it made when he lit it and the faint, lingering smell of gas after.

Father had a battered two-cup aluminium teapot. A rounded two-inch high tin in two sections. One for the loose tea the other for sugar. Milk came in a narrow bottle. Sweet-smelling sawdust gathered under his saw block. I ran my hands through it, smelling it as it fell silently through my fingers. Back in the classroom I spent the next three hour sneezing.

Ann took me home that first day. The bus dropped us off at the bottom of the Buncrana Road. 'Call in and see your uncle Fred,' Ann said, as we came up to the Lough Swilly Train Station. I've got to get home and help mother.'

I'd only seen my uncle Fred, father's brother, a few times when he'd call down to see father in our home. And when mother and I called in on our little strolls. He knew and saw me the moment I walked through the gate. He had his head bent under the open bonnet of a bus. The bus stood at a right angle to the gate.

A big smile lit up his oil-streaked face. He looked like an older edition of father. 'How's school?' he said. I told him about the recorder and the McDaids'. He pressed a sixpence into my hand when I left. 'Call in next week and see me.' said.

When I got home, mother asked me how was it? I told her that now I'd been to school I didn't need to go back again. I got one of mother's wry smiles at this. 'Did you see your uncle Fred?' she said.

Ann continued to take me to and from school for the next week or so. 'Then you're on your own. 'You're a big boy now,' she said, tousling my hair and rubbing my cheek with her soft warm hand.

'It's healthier for you to now go to school on your own,' mother said, backing Ann up. I remembered that phrase, 'more healthy' as used to keep me from sleeping in mother's big warm bed. What was it being used to keep me from now?

After that I then made my own way to school. Passing through Brooke Park, stopping, now and then, to look at glossy speckled fish lurking under huge water lilies in the Park's pond. The big library, always closed as I came and went to school

After school I made my own way home. Getting a bus at the Asylum road, down to the British Navy base. Then walking the rest of the way. Walking this last stretch, I called in once a week to see uncle Fred.

Once, on my way home from school, coming down the steep hill of Claradon Street, not far from the 'wee Nuns' in Francis Street, I fell, hitting my ear on the edge of coping stone in a garden wall.

Blood spurted from the lobe of my ear, ran down my cheek and onto my white short-sleeved shirt. I lay there dazed. Some stranger gathered me up and carried me the hundred yards to the Infirmity on the Northern Road. They stopped the bleeding. Plastered up my ear. I made my way home to a shocked mother.

'What in God's name's happened to you?' After that mother put Ann back on detail.

'I can manage on my own,' I said.

'You'll do as you're told, when you're told,' mother said. And the first thing you'll do is have a few days of school. I'll get Ann to call up and tell Mr Duffy what's happened.'

There was no way I was going to argue with that. Mother kept me off school for three days. I started back the following Monday. Ann on detail for the next two weeks.

My first day away from school was Wednesday. Brewster's bread van always called on a Wednesday. That's the day when mother had her little weekly treat. Before I'd started school it was my little treat as well. Two cupcakes and two small apple tarts. The apple tarts were for me. But we used to mix and match. As good a treat as the Saturday night toffees.

After having been in numerous houses, in the Marlborough Road area with father, he moved back to the workshop on Bishop Street. On our last day together he gave me the portable radio. And I stumbled upon 'American Forces Network' late that night to hear jazz for the first time.

A clarinet player, Sydney Bechet. I'd never heard a sound like that before. I remembered the sound of the piccolo at my aunt's. But this sound was very different. The piccolo was strangely beautiful and uplifting. It made me just want to sit very still and listen, without knowing what it was I was listening to.

But Bechet's clarinet playing, so relaxed, sweeping effortlessly up, down, up and away like one of father's kites. This was something else I'd found for myself that wasn't taught at school. I was hooked. Michael and Frank, my two brothers, sleeping in the same bedroom, woke up together. 'How are we supposed to get asleep with that din?' I turned the volume down and buried myself under the 'blankets' and turned against the wall.

There were no jazz bands in Derry in the early fifties, at least none I knew of. Even if there had there's no way they could possibly play like Bechet.

I told father I'd like to learn to play the clarinet. He came up with the idea of me joining the Saints Columb's Temperance Association Brass and Reed Band. He said he'd have a word with Jimmie McDaid. Four weeks later I was playing a major scale, DOH, Re, Mi, Fa, Sol, La, Ti, DOH, on one of the band's clarinets.

Practicing took place in St. Columb's hall. Not in the actual hall itself but underneath it. I travelled there by bus on my own, just as I'd gone to school on my own. Mother was pleased to think she had a budding musician in the family. Father was pleased because of the 'Temperance' side of the band hoping I'd follow in his dinosaur footprints and take the pledge not to drink alcohol.

It was in St. Columb's hall that I heard a Derry man

play jazz on a trumpet. He was a big fan of Louis Armstrong. The blaring loudness of the trumpet the vibrato rattling the windows. The thrill of that suspended beat. 'This music is the music of the young,' he said.

'Jimmie McDaid told me that after a few weeks, once you've shown you want to keep at it, you can take your clarinet home and practice at home as well.' father said.

'Where?' I said. I remembered what happened when I brought the bagpipes home.

'I'll clear a bit of the coal shed for you,' father said, after a bit of thought.

'You know you'll have to take the pledge to stay in band. All members of the band have taken the pledge. They're all tee-totelers, not one drinker among them.' Father was keen for me to take the 'pledge'. I could see that.

'OK, I said. I'd have said OK if he'd told me I'd first have to do a stint with 'Father Damien' in one of his leper colonies

The full force of the 'Temperance' end of the ban – absence from all alcohol – came to the fore when we played at a Gallic football match in Moville, over the border in the Republic. Twelve men, Jimmie McDaid and his two sons and me.

We marched around the pitch, playing the 'Soldier's Song', in our distinctive black uniforms. Each uniform displaying in gold lettering on the right hand side of the jacket the name of our band, St. Columb's Temperance Band. The spectators warmly applauded our playing. They stood behind a pegged rope that travelled around the perimeter of the field. A good few had Guinness bottles to their heads. If we'd played the Soldiers Song in Derry we'd have been arrested for sedition.

The players ran out onto the pitch, the spectators clapping and shouting, 'come on the wee Harps, come on Moville,' five minutes after we'd marched off it.

We retreated to the hut the players used to change. Inside all the men, but one, immediately took off their distinctive band uniform jackets. They piled them on the bench the players sat on and placed their instruments on top of their discarded jackets.

The two brothers kept theirs on but laid their instrument down. They must have known something I didn't. I started to take off my jacket.

' No, no, no', Jimmie McDaid said. You leave yours on, like my two boys.'

'Why?'

'Because.'

'Because what?' I said.

'Listen to me,' he said, grabbing me, digging his dirty fingernails into my shoulder. You do as you're told when you're told.'

Not something I haven't heard before. Jimmie could see I wasn't in the least impressed with all this.

'I'll deal with you when we get back,' he said, rising and pointing his index finger at me.

I opened my mouth to say...

'Best you keep your mouth shut now Boyle,' Jimmie said, lifting that index finger of his again.

I was silent for a moment. Then I put my hand up as I would do in the classroom if I wanted to ask a question.

Jimmie looked at me. 'You *are* a smart arse Boyle, even with your mouth shut.'

'Back from where?' I said.

The one man who hadn't taken off his jacket, Freddie McLaughlin, said to those who had, 'All right lads, cough up.' As the jacketless men filed out of the hut, some pressed a sixpence coin into his outstretched hand others tossed it at him.

I couldn't make out what was going on. As the two brothers didn't bat an eyelid I supposed they'd seen all this before. But seen all what? As soon as they'd all gone the two brothers headed for the door picking up their clarinets as the went.

'Where are you pair going?' I said.

'They're going to watch the match, and so are you,' Freddie said. I'm staying here to keep an eye on our stuff'.'

I picked up my clarinet and once outside, I stalled to tie my shoelace. The brothers went on. I came around to the other side of the hut to see the last of the men stepping over a fallen bull-wire fence. I followed the worn track across the field. On reaching the fence there was no sign of any of them. Where had they gone and why had they gone in the first place?

'What a bunch of 'tossers', to use the father's descriptive phrase of the card, pitch, and toss contingent, they are,' I thought.

I stepped over the fence down onto a main road. Followed it for about a hundred yards. On the right hand side of the road was a big house. The door was open. I walked in to hear a lot of loud laughter. There they were. All of them sitting on high stools drinking Guinness out of bottles.

Jimmie McDaid turned on his stool when the barman said, 'What are you doing in here with that Temperance uniform on?'

'What are they doing in here without their Temperance uniforms?' I said.

'You are a smart arse, Boyle,' Jimmie said. Then on reflection, 'No you're not at all a smart arse John.' He'd never called me 'John' before. He'd be calling me 'Johnnie' any minute now. 'Come here,' he said.

The bartender opened his mouth to protest, but Jimmie raised his index finger at him. 'Mind your business bartender.'

The bartender fell silent. 'Give the young fella a glass of lemonade bartender,' Jimmie said. Bit more to our Jimmie boy than meets the eye.

'Can you play that thing?' said the bartender as I came up to the bar.

I took a swig of the lemonade. Wet the reed of my clarinet with my saliva and played a bit of the 'Soldier's Song'. The bar fell silent as I played. Republicans all.

A round of applause followed this. Further up the bar I heard a voice say, 'Well done Boyle.' Out pops Quinn's big head. His nose now inflamed with all the little capillary joined up 'Well done Boyle', he said again as he staggered towards me, his stool hitting the bar floor with a crash.

'Leave the boy alone, Quinn,' said Jimmie as he gets off his stool. Pick up your stool and get back on it before I put you back on it. Now, he said, turning to me, you run along back like a good little boy (at least it wasn't 'Hello Little Boy') John and watch the match. And I promise, as everyone else here does – looking around the bar his index finger raised – and that includes you Quinn – not to tell your father you've been in a public house.'

There was more to Jimmie boy than I'd first thought. He'd the making of a politician in him.

Just before half time they all appeared again the worst for wear. They donned their jackets, gathered up their instruments. The players were coming off the field too, 'Well done the wee Harps'.

The band marched out onto the pitch. Jimmie McDaid beckoned us three boys to join them. Off we all went around the pitch playing 'Danny Boy'.

But this time is was different. The men were all out of step. Three or four of them tripped over. Got up and started looking at the ground to find out what it was they'd tripped over when it was their own feet.

.And, 'Danny Boy' was being played so badly that the crowd started to boo and throw sods of earth at us and the odd, empty, Guinness bottle.

In total disarray now the individual band members stampeded back to the coach. A group of Guinness-bottle wielding spectators followed them. Sods of earth continued to reign down on them.

I stood to one side. Jimmie's two sons joined the players running for the bus looking as though this was 'par for the course' for them wherever the band played.

As the men tried to push through the door of the coach the fighting began even before the Guinness bottle-wielding spectators got to the bus. Jimmie lashed out at one of the trumpet players as they fought to get through the door of the bus. Two trombone players were lying on the ground having punched one another trying to get to the front of this now motley band. It was a right shamble.

On the journey home a row started at the front of the bus. Four or five members of the band surrounded Freddy McLaughlin. One leaned across and smacked Freddie's head with the flat of his big hand. The driver stopped the bus.

'Unless you lot all sit down and be quiet I'll dump you here and you can find your own way home.'

In the back of the bus Quinn lolling about in his seat kept saying' Well done Boyle.' Well done...'

School Pennyburn

In 1954, St Patricks Primary school in Pennyburn opened and I said good riddance to Rosemount. No more starting out at 7:30 in the morning. No more buses to get to school our new school a five-minute walk from home.

Mr. Quinn, our music teacher, he of the nose, who'd, taught me music at Rosemount school lived in Troy Park just off the Culmore Road. No more travelling for him either as he transferred to St. Patricks.

One of the most friendly and jovial men was a Mr. Flanagan the Art teacher. A big hulk of a man with a wavy shock of jet-black hair, a jazzy brown lounge suit. He always seemed to have his hands in his trouser pockets. Playing with loose change or something. Later I decided he wasn't playing with no loose change. I'd have heard it jingle. I decided that he was playing 'pocket billiards' to keep his testosterone levels up.

It was Brian Friel who'd the task of schooling us for the 11+ exam. His piercing little dark eyes seemed always to be observing, watching, seeing over and above what was needed for his teaching.

He'd come to my desk when he thought I wasn't either paying enough attention or to encourage me to better results. He'd use his bony finger joints to punch, gently, my arm muscles.

Mr. McDermott, the head teacher, would come into our class to give us all a pep talk about the importance of this 11+. He was most certainly not singing to the choir as far as I was concerned. My head was filled with all manner of things. I was ablaze with energy, completely locked into my home surroundings and myself. I was at home in our back lanes and streets as an otter is in water, melting into my surroundings.

McDermott had false teeth. He'd turn an empty desk around, sit on the desktop, his feet where his bum should have been. By design, or accident, every time he came into our class, he'd place himself directly opposite the desk I sat at.

As he spoke, spittle would lash my face and the face of the boy behind me. And maybe the boy behind him. He didn't bat an eyelid. He must have thought we'd be privileged to be spat on by such as he.

It was in Friel's best interests to see that as many of us passed this 11+ exam, as it would reflect well on his ability as a teacher. Leading up to this exam, we were asked by Friel to write a composition about anything we either liked or felt strongly about. I wrote about father.

How he was a cabinet maker and joiner. A quiet man of few words, smoke signals were louder by comparison, who did his talking with the tools of his trade. A language that was to me, as a boy of three, a completely new sweetness, like mother's milk. How I sniffed the soft scent of the pine-wood as he made a drop-side cot for my brother Michael. And smelt the animal glue heating on the polished range. Listened to the prolonged clean sound of his smoothing plane as it dressed the wood to a glossy silkiness, the shavings like coiled bangles.

The honest buzz and burr of his 'Disston' hand saw cutting through seasoned timber. The little dust mites of sawdust sinking and gathering on the floor. And floating in the air, making me sneeze and rub my nose. A habit I still have today, with or without sawdust.

I wrote that when sawing, he always kept his thumb pressed lightly against the blade of his saw. This so he was in touch with the wood and his saw and, practically, kept the cut straight. Distracted once he nicked his thumb. Medallions of blood slow motioned into the sawdust below thickening it into a mealy paste.

He wetly licked his thumb, stooped, causally, down, and pressed it still bleeding into this mealy paste. After a little while he picked up his saw and carried on.

I remember Friel read my composition out to the class. He didn't read any of the others out.

Bill McCoy, an officer in the United States Navy, stationed at Clooney Road Barracks in the Waterside, Derry, had a girlfriend called Mary Gallagher. She lived with her mother and father in St. Francis Terrace where, in the back lane, I watched men playing cards and pitch and toss on a Sunday after Mass. It was the last house in the terrace and overlooked a small stream that ran into a bigger stream running through 'Kelly's field' and on into the river Foyle.

Kelly's Field' were we children played in the long, endless, summer days. Jumping across this stream was a competitive game for boys and girls. I always lost. Every time I jumped across I always fell backwards into the stream. I'd land alright, but when I straightened up I'd lose my balance and fall into the stream. That dizzy head thing again which I'd had since a child.

I wasn't bothered about my wet clothes. They weren't mine. But once I fell in when I'd a new pair of boots mother had bought especially for me on my birthday. I had to sneak back into the house and when no one was watching, I stuffed my wet boots with old newspapers.

I then stuck them in the range oven to dry out. Mother pulled them from the oven with a pair of coal tongs after the paper caught fire. Dumped them into the Belfast sink and turned the tap on them making them more wet than they'd been the first time.

'That was a good idea,' she said. Stuffing your boots with newspapers. Just don't put them in the oven the next time.'

Mary Gallagher was a big friend of my sister Bridy. They used to get 'dolled up' together in our house to go dancing at 'The Criterion' (The Crit' they called it.) On Foyle Street, just along from the Guildhall, where Brian Friel's play, 'Translations' was performed in 1980.

One Sunday after watching a card game, instead of going my usual way home I went the opposite way, heading for the back of 22 Francis Terrace. As I approached, I heard a thwacking, pinging noise.

As I stuck my head around the corner, I saw a man sitting on the high back-garden wall, his long legs dangling over. He'd an .22 air rifle raised to his shoulder shooting at light bulbs placed on a rock in the stream.

Lying beneath him were huge cigarette butts, some still smouldering. I counted six. He wore a pair of bright blue jeans, a gleaming white 'T' shirt, a pair of shoes with no laces, and a United States Navy 'Dixie Cup' hat cocked to one side. He'd a cigarette at the side of his mouth from which, as I looked, he took a puff, then flicked it into the back lane using his thumb and middle finger. I watched, mesmerized.

I heard the first growlings of thunder, then an almighty explosion and a big flash of lighting. The heavy drops of rain, staining my Sunday white shirt went torrential. The cigarette butts turning to messy liquid shreds.

McCoy jumps down from the wall, up the lane he runs onto the tarmac of the pavement. I follow. Now he's dancing along the pavement, the rain beating into him. He takes not a blind bit of notice. He's swinging out of the street lamp posts. Now he's singing; 'I'm singing in the rain, what a wonderful feeling, I'm happy...'

And just as suddenly as the rain started, it stopped. I shook my head and looked up. McCoy's still sitting on the wall and I hear the dry zips of his air gun as another light bulb is smashed to smithereens. There're now eight butts in the lane, two still smouldering. All crisp and dry.

McCoy smoked 'Lucky Strike' and 'Chesterfield' cigarettes. But not like we did, he didn't. We sucked our 'Park Drive' cigarettes down to the last shred of tobacco, burning our fingers as we did.

I picked up all the butts after he'd gone inside and stowed them in my jacket pocket. I said nothing to anyone where I'd got the them.

The only time I saw a cigarette was Saturday, when father gave me sixpence pocket money. I'd pay three pence to get in to see a movie at the British Legion hut on the Collin lane. And two and a half pence bought me one Park Drive cigarette from Goodman's shop across the street from St. Patrick's Terrace. The only shop in Pennyburn then.

The following Monday afternoon at about 3:30 when school was over, I hared it down the Racecourse Road to the back lane of St. Francis Terrace. And there again were these huge butts, about seven or eight of them.

I'd tidy these butts up, removing dead ash, and flicking back lane dust of them and put them into one of father's empty 'John Players' cigarette boxes. Take them to school. In the playground the next day, I'd sell them on for a penny each, just as I'd done with the first lot.

One day in class, my John Players cigarette box, full of these butts, went missing. I put my hand into my jacket pocket and they weren't there. I quickly searched my other pockets. No sign. Then I remembered I'd had a bit of a run in with big Jimmie Duffy as we came into the classroom that morning. He'd grabbed a hold of me demanding to know where I got the butts.

'Come on Boyle,' where are you getting them?'

'Leave off Jimmy', I said, pulling away from him as Friel looked over the top of his spectacles at the pair of us. 'You're going to get us both hammered.'

Duffy was two desks behind me. When Friel's back was turned to the blackboard, I turned pointing at Duffy. 'You've got my fags.'

'No, I don't,' he said, burying his head in the book on his desk. Something I'd never seen him do before.

I got out of my desk just as Friel turned.

"Going somewhere Boyle,' he said.

'Duffy's stolen my cigarettes, sir,' I said.

Friel put down the chalk on the fluted bottom of the blackboard and sat down at his desk. 'Both of you up here, now,' he said.

' I told you Duffy, were both in for it now,' I said as we approached Friel's table.

'Out with it Boyle,' said Friel.

I told him the story about the American sailor, Bill McCoy, who often visited a friend of Bridy's, my sister, Mary Gallagher. She lived in the end house of St. Francis Terrace, in Pennyburn. I told him McCoy had a.22 air rifle. And how he'd place light bulbs on a rock in the stream and sitting up on the high wall of the back garden shoot at them, flicking these huge butts onto the lane in between times.

I told him I only got one cigarette a week, bought at 'Goodman's' the only shop in Pennyburn, when father give me my pocket money the rest spent at the British Legion Hall in the Collin lane, run by ex British Servicemen from Messings Park, where they showed moving pictures every Saturday and where I smoked my one cigarette.

Friel didn't once try to interrupt as I talked. Neither did those in the class who smoked. But I could see Friel was listening intently his little dark eyes gleaming. Not glistening, like I remembered the sailor boy's in our back lane.

'That a well told little tale Boyle,' he said after I'd stopped talking. What moving pictures do you watch at the British Legion hut?'

'Superman', 'Laurel and Hardy' and sometimes 'Hop-along Cassidy,' I said.

Turning to Duffy he said, 'Empty your pockets on the table Duffy, now.' The John Players cigarette packet landed on Friel's desk. Opening the packet, Friel turned the content out onto his desk. 'These yours Boyle?' he said.

I told him they were.

'Do you smoke them all yourself?

I said I sold them for a penny each in the playground.

'Well, said Friel, there'll be no selling today Boyle. Or any other day in the school. You do your selling after school.' He put the John Players packet into his desk top.

Now that it was common knowledge where I'd got the huge butts it was just a question of who got to the back lane first. Smart arse that I am, I still had a trick left up my sleeve. I told Bridy about the butts. She had a word on Mary. Mary had a word on McCoy. This puts an end to the cigarette butts in the back lane.

The following week I came to school with a full un-opened pack of twenty 'Lucky Strike', curtsey of McCoy, through the good offices of Mary and my sister Bridy. I sold fifteen of these to the picture goers the following Saturday at twopence each.

* * *

Despite Friel's best efforts, I failed my 11+ exam and started my apprenticeship as a shop joiner with McLaugh and Hall on Bishop Street when I was fourteen.

The workshop was beside a bacon-curing factory with the glorious smell of bacon in the air all day long. The last time I tasted bacon it was Christmas, six months ago. But it didn't beat the pleasure I found in the simple smell of wood.

One day coming out of the workshop with the yard labourer, each pushing one of the long handle of a handcart on our way down to 'Keys, Builders' Merchants on the Strand Road I chanced into Friel..

He stopped, looked at me, then the handcart. He reached out his thin bony hand and shook mine.' Is this what you wanted? He said.

'No, it's not,' I said.

'Good luck Boyle, he said. He continued on down Bishop Street, most likely on his way to St. Columb's College, just opposite the Nazareth House were the 'wee Nuns' are. 'The Sisters of Nazareth'.

I never saw Friel again until October 1968. The Saturday after the then, Royal Ulster Constabulary baton-charged the Civil Rights marchers in Derry. He was in a crowd outside the Guildhall with a hanky tied around his jacket to show he was one of the stewards. I always loved the connection between him and father. A wordy connection admittedly, Friel a playwright father a shipwright.

Although not seeing Friel again after 1968 I read about his success as a playwright. In particular, I remember his 'Translations' in the Guildhall in Derry in 1980.

And I thought then that we, the indigenous Irish of Derry, didn't need a history lesson, but adequate social housing that wasn't 'Gerrymandered' by the Derry Corporation. That was my first ignorant impression.

In later years when I read Friel's 'Translations' I found it deeply moving and culturally relevant. The deliberate, ruthless destruction of our language by the Anglicization of

93

the Irish map for military purposes.

At the heart of 'Translations', there's a lack of bitterness against the English engaged in this destruction. However, Friel managed brilliantly to display the arrogance of the English in Ireland at that time. But he knew what was happening was inevitable. And today, I'm glad I speak English. And all Friel's successful works are in English. But language does not determine nationality. Sentiment does.

Boom Hall (1)

Some time after the death of my aunt, my two brothers, Michael, Frank and I set out from Boom Hall. It was late August. We walked down the Buncrana Road, passed St. Patricks Chapel. I didn't say a word about St. Patrick. We made a left at the bottom onto the Culmore Road.

'Do you know where this Boom Hall is?' said Frank.

'Of course I do,' I said. Over this stone boundary wall, down to the air raid shelter, then follow the river Foyle.'

"Who told...?'

'My aunt Gertrude,' I said. 'Let's go.'

'Your aunt Gertrude?' said Michael.

They both ran ahead. I followed by a slightly different route having been here before. But for a different reason. A short distance beyond the air raid shelter in a copse of trees, I saw two figures moving about on a big overcoat the arms twisted at an angle. Like a horizontal scarecrow in a field of green corn.

As I got closer I could hear grunts and groans. The two figures were one bundled together as they were. As I approached a medley of clothes turned towards me. It was a man and a woman. They were both sweating.

'Hey, little boy,' said the man. Run back to the shop on the Culmore Road, and get us some lemonade, or anything to drink. It's worth a sixpence to you.' He flicks the sixpence at me. 'That's yours. This is for the lemonade.' He flicked the shilling.

95

I looked at the pair of them lying there. I thought of the girl I used to bump into on the swing and how good it felt. But I didn't like the 'Hi little boy', bit.

'Go get your own lemonade,' I said, dropping both coins on the crumpled overcoat. I'm off to Boom Hall.'

I caught up with my brothers. 'Where've you been?'

The tide was out, the sun glittering on the black glar. The homes of American servicemen, on the other side of the river, each a different cardinal colour, stood out like grounded rainbows against the drab grey of the Du Point factory.

There were dozens of tiny gravely inlets where the river had eroded the grassy banks. We jumped from bank to the gravel from gravel to bank. After about an hour I spotted the avenue of trees.

'This is it,' I said

'How'd you know?' said Frank.

'I know.'

Nothing moved in the eerie silence. We clambered over the boundary wall. Up the avenue of trees. We climbed hearing a faint trickle of running water as it made its way down to the river. Ten, maybe fifteen minutes of climbing brought us to the end of the avenue of trees. Spread out before us a short grassy bank. Ahead of us, huge chestnut trees.

And just as my aunt said chestnuts shaped like pears, no spikes and coloured grey And big. But not yet ready. They'd be ready when the winds of October came. We sauntered up to the chestnut trees. They were in a great circle.

Our lowered voices echoed, bouncing of the trunks of the tress and up into the empty blue sky. Empty but for a few gulls drifting silently on the thermals.

We mooched around for a while, then pushed on and came to a long run of unbroken high hawthorn trees two or three feet in depth. Frank found the 'scoot hole'. Or what had once had been a 'scoot hole'. Frank had an eye for 'scoot holes'.

He battled his way through. We followed. Clear of the hawthorn trees, we came up against a red-bricked wall with crumbling mortar joints covered in ivy. It was some ten-foot high.

About a foot or so above the wall we saw the tops of pear-laden trees. We followed the makings of a narrow path between the hawthorn and the wall looking for a way in. We didn't find one.

Following the wall running at a right angle to the main wall we came to where the hawthorn trees ceased. Thick overgrown ivy clung to this wall too. We looked down its length. In the distance we could see Boom Hall house. It looked deserted. Off to the left of the house, a thick copse of pine trees.

'Is that smoke rising above those trees?' Frank said.

Retreating to where we'd first started, Frank, shrugging his shoulders said, 'You two stay put.' I'm going to start looking again. Makes no sense. Must be an entrance somewhere.' His dander was up at not finding an entrance.

After about a half hour or so on his own he found it. An old ledged, braced and sheeted patchy-green painted door buried behind where the ivy was thickest on the first wall we came across.

The rusty bolt was on our side. Michael, with a piece of a branch, belted and tapped the bolt clear, pulled the door open. The big 'T' hinges screeched in protest their sound dry chalk across the school blackboard.

Pear trees, pinned back against the wall, laden with fruit. Swathes of strawberries lay stretched before us. There was no sound but the buzz of insects, the twittering of birds. Laden apple trees, ripe as the pears.

They all looked untouched. Little man-made paths crisscross this cultivated paradise. We entered a huge timber green house half-full of ripe tomatoes, the other half full of low plum trees with white powdery blue fruit. Just like the ones my aunt used to bring down on a Wednesday night. The pungent, fruity smell of the greenhouse overwhelmed us. We recognised the gooseberry bushes, having occasionally raided Father Glackens's parochial house garden full of gooseberries.

Here were all manner of berries, blue, red, orange. We'd never seen the like. We didn't ever know if all the berries were eatable.

Once of twice we thought we'd heard someone cough. The sound of quiet muttering, at which we stopped dead looking at one another. But nobody appeared. Even though we'd spotted, what looked like a recently built lean-to hut built against the wall from where we'd seen the big house, when we first entered the garden.

We took off our trouser belts, belted them over our waist of our pullovers, and crammed them with apples and pears. Our stomachs bulging we blundered from the garden pulling the screeching door behind us, drawing the bolt, resettling the ivy as best we could.

'We'll be back here again, that's for sure,' Frank said. We need to make certain we don't tell anybody about this. And especially not where the entrance is.'

We made our way back to the Culmore Road stopping at the air raid shelters to adjust our belts and have a pee. Waiting for my brothers, I remembered the slingshot wars I'd fought in these same air raid shelters.

We'd split into two groups of five or six boys. I'd lead one group. Mosey Brown, who later became a Christian brother, the other, both of us thought of as the best of slingshot-war tacticians.

Once Mosey out-tacticianed me. I stumbled into him dodging a blitz of gravel the size of seagulls' eggs from the other boys on Mosey's side. His sling shot up and partly drawn, mine loosely at my side. He looked at me. I looked at him. 'Ah, Jesus Moses,' I said. You wouldn't, not at such close range.'

He hesitated for a moment.

'Blessed are the merciful, for they shall obtain mercy,' I said. I'd heard Father Glackin say that one.

Mosey, giving me one of his manish up-from-under looks said, 'You're wasting your sweetness on the desert air Boyle.'

'He's been listening to our music teacher Quinn,' I thought.

He pulled his sling shot back to its full extent. Then lowered it down to the level of my trouser pocket, this full of different sized gravel, and let fly. The stone smashed into my pocket.

'Always be prepared for the unexpected Boyle,' he said. Next time I'll take your big smart-arse head off.' Then he was gone. My bruised blue leg, the bruise the size of my trouser pocket, throbbed for a week.

We were wild, savage. The bomb that St. Patrick had directed into the sand pit opposite the chapel unearthed a great gravel pit. Here was an endless supply of slingshot ammunition. And the wars of the air raid shelter relocated to this sand pit.

Here we split one another's heads open. Split heads, we carried with pride. It wasn't only our own heads we split. The sound of a blackbird or thrush drew us like a siren call. The clunk of the bird head as a sling shot stone tore it off.

We Irish Catholics in Northern Ireland – we called it North Ireland – in the 50's, were estranged from our surroundings. Cut off as we were from our hinterland of Donegal in the Irish Republic. The oppressive nature of policing. The gerrymandering in jobs and housing. The threatening beat

99

of the Orangemen's' drums on the 12th. July. Their placards 'Keep Ulster Protestant' a reminder that we were not wanted here. And from this, our internecine sling shot wars as we turned in on ourselves as a prelude to turning out of those same selves.

'Come on, let's go,' I said to my brothers. We clambered up the bank toward the wall we'd a few hours ago jumped over. Two policemen were leaning on the wall. Their black patrol car, engine , idling on the other side of the road.

There were another two older boys in the back of the car – both of whom looked familiar

'Jesus, said Michael. Where'd they come from?'

'Do you know those two in the back of the car?' Frank said.

'What's up you jumpers?' one of the policemen said.

'Down our jumpers,' I said.

'John, shut up,' said Michael. Pay no attention to him Mr, we always addressed the police as Mister, He's just a bit of a smart arse.'

'OK smart arse, what's down your jumpers?'

These were two grown men in full police uniform, each with a baton in a black leather case, a polished holster with a thick cord looped into the revolver butt. And they were questioning us about apples and pears?

'We've been working for the McDivvits at Boom Hall. And they paid us with apples and pears, that's what's down our jumpers,' I said.

Michael and Frank went quiet at this.

'You've a lot to say for yourself haven't you?' What school do you all go to?' said the younger policeman.

We all knew what that meant.

'We're Catholics,' I said.

'Right, over the wall you come.' We'll all take a nice drive down and see the McDivvits. Let them tell us what you've just told us.'

I wasn't too sure if the police car could make it down the private road to McDivvits. It probably couldn't. And if we got into the police car we'd know who the other two boys were. But... I looked at Michael and Frank. 'Run for it.' We ran as best we could back to the air raid shelter and along its length. I glanced back. The policemen didn't jump over the wall. They just watch us run.

We ran towards Garden City, crossed the Culmore road, through Troy Park, where Frank, the scoot whole king' had previously found a scoot that got us back into our own territory.

We scrambled through the hole. The same two policemen were waiting. We were too tired to run further. Someone had told them about our scoot hole. It could have only been someone in our territory. A police informer.

'We've been here before,' the younger policemen said.

'Who told you about our scoot hole?' I said.

'Scoot' hole is it, said the older policeman, looking at the other. That's a good name for it, 'Scoot' hole', I'll have to remember that one.'

'Look, I said, we were frightened when we told you we were Catholics.' That's why we ran away. It wasn't as if we'd anything to hide. If you still want to take us down to see the McDivvits, we're all happy to go.' I looked at Michael and Frank. They said nothing.

' I'll tell you what boys, you can keep your pears and apples this time, but if we ever catch you again, with whatever's up or down your jumpers, you're all for the long jumpers,' he said.

I could see the younger policeman about to protest at this. But the older policeman leaned over and whispered in his ear. Maybe the older policeman knew that they couldn't drive down there this time of year. Or maybe he didn't want

101

us to find out who the other two older boys were in the back of his police patrol car.

Boom Hall (2)

In October, Frank, Michael and I, made it back to Boom Hall. This time we travelled by the private road that my aunt had asked me not to take. She never told me why.

'Why didn't we come this way the first time?' said Michael. 'Because my aunt asked me not to,' I said. And I'd promised her I wouldn't.'

'What's all this 'my aunt' business,' said Frank. She was our aunt too.'

I told them she'd asked to see me on my first communion day. And that we'd got on well. That she'd asked, insisted, that I didn't use the road she did when she was working for the McDivvits.

'So, what's changed now?' Frank said.

'Well', I said, 'she asked 'me'. Now it's 'we.' '

'Smart arse as usual,' said Michael.

As we travelled along its length we slung the odd big tree branch into the hedgerows the road strewn with debris as our aunt had said. Here and there we clambered over a fallen tree.

My aunt had told me that this private road leads directly to McDivvit's house. She'd never said why she didn't want me to use it. When we came to where we could see the house in the distance I spotted a sidetrack.

'I think it's better we steer clear of the house, just in case someone's there,' I said. We singled-filed our way down this side track. It leads directly into the grassy bank at the top of the avenue of trees we'd followed up from the shore the last time.

The October wind had done its job. Fallen chestnuts littered the ground encased in their partially open shells brought about by their fallen contact with the earth.

Once fully unshelled their burnished brownness shone with an erotic gleam. Like something so new and strange they might have fallen from a passing meteorite.

It was as though each individual chestnut came equipped with its own internal polishing brush. The final polish done in the expectation of the October winds bringing them to the ground. There to lie half-opened. A partially open treasure chest waiting for us.

At Technical College, years later, I learned of a prismatic compass, used to show the position of a ship at sea. I thought it would show the exact position of the ship. But it didn't. It only showed it as 'near enough'. It wasn't perfect. Which was what I was looking for, something beautiful, something perfect, something unalterable. At that first moment of fully opening the pear-like shell of the fallen chestnut, I'd found that perfection, that momentary unalterableness. Flawless in its burnished brown depth. But not for long.

These burnished brown jewels of chestnuts would end up in the range oven to dry out. And emerge shrunken, cratered and wrinkled. Toughened and hard as nails ready to do battle in the schoolyard.

Halfway up the trees, even bigger chestnuts, not yet fallen, beckoned. And the stick I threw up to dislodge them all those years ago has still not reached the ground, caught as it is now in the trees myriad branches and twigs.

We again venture around to the hidden garden. Pushed back the ivy and entered carrying the chestnuts in the cloth bags we'd brought with us. Everything was gone. The orchard stripped clean. Wasps buzzing around some rotted pear and apples lying on the ground, strawberries, all berries gone. An empty green house.

'Jesus, Frank said, what's happened here?'

We stopped on hearing the bolt shot closed on the gate. We scrambled back. Frank shouldered it, but to no avail.

'"We'll have to climb the wall, look for a ladder or rope or something,' said Frank, as he again tried to shoulder the gate open.

'Who's closed the gate, that's the question?' said Michael. We found neither ladder nor rope.

'So you're back,' said a voice behind us. It was my aunt's old posh accent. But more rounded, clear, distinct, spoken as though the speaker really did have plums in her mouth.

She stood there, a tall swaying figure, a woollen shawl hanging over her narrow shoulders, a long, green dress with daisy chains on it and black patented leather shoes. Her hair, a halo of black tinged with grey. Her eyes mackerel, blue.

'I could call the police, have you arrested, trespassing, talking my pears and apples,' she said.

'We didn't know anyone was here.' We thought the place empty. We never saw anyone. We'd heard that the place had gone to wrack and ruin,' I said.

'Where'd you hear that?' she said.

I looked at Michael and Frank. 'Tell her where you heard it,' Michael said.

'My aunt.

'Aunt?'

'Aunt Gertrude,' I said.

'Aunt Gertrude?' What's your name?'

'McDaid,' said Frank, looking at the pair of us.

Something about her, though... 'I could call the police' she'd said. And her relaxed presence in front of we three boys. 'It's Boyle,' I said.

Behind us I heard a wheelbarrow moving on the gravelled path. Over my shoulder I saw a stooped black-haired man. He skirted slowly round us. Then turned the barrow and stood facing us. He had an earring in his right ear, tall, broad-shouldered, his hair pitch black. He wore a pair of dungarees.

'Was it your aunt who told you about the orchard?' She said.

'No. She only told us about the chestnut trees. And not to go near the big house,' I said.

They looked at one another. 'How would you like to help out?' Jason could do with a hand to tidy things up around here,' she said.

'You're not going to call the police?' I said.

'We'll see.'

They both turned, strolled back a little down the gravelled path. She looked over her shoulder at us. Had a little chat. We couldn't hear what they were saying. Back they came.

'You come with me,' she said, pointing a long slender finger at me. You two help Jason. There's compost to be made, burning to be done. When you're finished Jason will bring you over to the house.'

I shrugged my shoulders, lifted my head held my hands out, palms up and nodded at Michael and Frank. 'She's not calling the police, right?'

' Jesus,' said Frank, did you see that man's face?'

The lean-to hut had a corrugated iron roof and a big deadlocked pitch-pine door. She unlocked it with a key she took from her dress pocket. The door opened out. She reached round and pulled a light switch.

Dozens of small timber crates lay ramshackle up on top of each other against each wall. We crossed the dirt floor.

Another big pitch-pine door. She unlocked it with the same key. We were on the lawn of Bloom Hall. I turned to see her close this door. Fixed in some way to this side of the door, thick ivy.

The house was over three stories, topped by a bell tower. All the windows had closed internal shutters from the first floor up, the ground floor window sashes open at the bottom slightly. In these ground floor rooms white sheets loosely covered furniture. An outside iron staircase leads up to a bell tower.

Set back in a thick copse of pine trees, a couple of hundred yards from the main house, a small one-storey building, built in similar fashion. She unlocked the front door and beckoned me in. I looked behind me as I entered. It was so still and silent. Huge chestnut trees surrounded the house. Partially opened chestnuts littered the ground. An old diesel lorry, tailgate down, and half filled with logs, stood under one of the chestnut trees. An axe head buried in a tree stump. It's long, elegantly shaped hickory shaft burnished with use to a glossy silkiness.

A log fire burnt in an old cast-iron fireplace, spinning sparks into the fine-mesh of a fireguard. Above the mantle piece two painted portraits, one either end. An elderly couple, he sitting, she standing behind him her hand on his shoulder.

Higher up, and equal distance between, another portrait. A young woman, again, sitting, her hands folded, resting on her lap. Her hair pitch black her eyes blue as the bluest sky. The red-tiled hearth was under a thin film of white ash. A low murmur of indistinct music swelled softly from a wireless. Then the sound of a piccolo.

She moved towards a Belfast sink below a small window, filled a big kettle, turned and puts it on the gas cooker. It made a 'whoosh' as she lit it.

'Would you like some tea?' she said. What's your first

name? I'm Patricia.'

Had I asked these questions it would have taken me two seconds to utter them. But it took her what felt to me like three minutes in that precise cut-glass accent of hers. Yet I liked it. It seemed to blend with and compliment the music.

'Yes, I said. 'John. Hello Patricia.'

She turned, her face lit up in a brief embracing smile. I felt a shiver run across my shoulders, down my back, down my legs. On the side wall there was a gas mantel. She puts a match to this. It too gives out a little 'whoosh'. The smell of gas from this lingered, hung in the air like a faint memory. It's little fishtail blue light threw shaky shadows across the room.

A gleaming round table with four green upholstered chairs sat on a large mat full of colours with tasselled sides and edges. The floor was dull, unpolished pitch pine in herringbone pattern. A large flower patterned dish full of plums sat on the table. A cot at the far end of the room full of timber crates. The drop side section had horizontal bars.

'I was sorry to hear about your aunt,' Patricia said, as she motioned me to sit at the table. She set some brown-coloured biscuits on the table on a small white delft plate and poured the boiling water into the delf teapot. She wrapped a woollen tea cosy around it.

'We had tea here together, your aunt and I, each day,' she said. Including the day she left.'

She'd liked my aunt. Wasn't annoyed that she'd been left the money by her parents.

'Where's all the fruit gone?' I said.

She told me that for the last five or six years, McLaughlin's men, ganged bossed by him, picked all the fruit for her. Put in crates and onto his boat. Took it all up to Derry where he sold it.

'The money we get is what we now live on'. And it's

paid to us before the men start picking the fruit.'

"Very business like,' I thought.

When Michael and Frank, came in with Jason she rose and beckoned them to the sink. There to wash their hands and come to the table for tea and biscuits.

'Would you like to have a look inside the big house John, while your brothers are having tea with Jason?'

Frank and Michael looked at me. Michael, with his hands held out, palms up, mouthed 'John?'

'I would Patricia.' I said.

She told me there was wet and dry rot in all but the ground floor rooms that she couldn't afford to treat. McLaughlin's men had moved all the furniture down to the ground floor.

'They're calling tomorrow to take it all in his boat up to Derry for sale at auction,' she said.

The rooms were huge. The ceilings high. And the blinds just as aunty had said, drawn up, the windows being so high. The blinds themselves must have looked magnificent in their heyday. Even now you could make out huge designs of once brilliantly coloured birds, peacocks and pheasants printed onto to them. Oak bookcases lined the walls of the main living room.

Where're all the books?' I said. Aunty told me that there were hundred and hundreds of books.'

'A house not lived in is no place for books. And I've done all the reading I intend.'

We had cast iron fireplaces at home. This fireplace, in the main room, with its convoluted embossed vines and arched ironwork, was as big as all our fireplaces put together. Either side of this fireplace were built-in cupboards fashioned in oak. The unprotected, once silky grain, now dark and sullen in its neglect.

'I'd asked aunty if she'd take me down to see the books, but she said she couldn't,' I said.

109

'Did she say why?'

'No.She didn't.'

'All the book are in the public library in Brook Park'. Do you read a lot John?'

'I've always read,' I said.

She looked straight at me. 'Go up to the library in a week or so, tell them who you are, they'll give you any of the books you want.'

Michael and Frank had finished their tea when we got back.

'Jason will show you the cellar where we've kept some of the fruit picked earlier for ourselves. Take what you can carry, she said. Not in your usual way, down your jumpers. There's shopping bags beside the cot, you can have those. And maybe next year you can all come and visit us again.'

'Why did your parents leave the money to our aunt?' I said.

Jason looked across at her, waiting for the answer.

'You are full of questions, aren't you John,' Patricia said.

She continued on without answering and told us that because she was paid 'up front' she sold all the fruit on favourable terms, allowing McLaughlin to make a good profit and pay his men They'd both learned, over the years, to trust one another. 'Dividing the money fairly builds trust,' she said.

This reminded me how Michael, Frank and I used to evenly divide the money from the selling of shamrocks. She was right about the 'trust'.

Jason walked us back to the path that lead to the Culmore Road. He didn't speak except when he pointed up the private road and said, 'Culmore Road.'

His accent was not that of hers. It was solemn, slow, like a father's farming family who lived in County Derry. Then he turned and went back to Patricia.

'Jesus Christ,' said Michael. Did you see the face on that man? Who in under God does he remind you of?'

'Let's not to there', I said.

'He's a lot younger than her,' said Frank.

'What got me as well is that we all sat around having tea and eating biscuits on my aunt's furniture,' I said.

We looked at one another. 'Something's going on here that it's maybe best we know nothing about,' said Michael.

'Let's go,' I said.

We set off up the private road with our cloth bags, full of chestnuts and three grocer's bags full to bursting with pears and apples.

'So, what's with all this 'John' and 'Patricia' stuff,' said Michael. How'd she know your first name and you hers?'

'She told me. I told her.'

'Thick as thieves you pair,' said Frank.

'No more thicker than we three thieves,' I said.

We clambered over the branches strewn across the road and climbed over fallen trees again. Michael was walking in front. He puts his hands out in front of him, palms up, and looked over his shoulder at us. 'Someone's coming,' he said.

We dived into the hedgerow bordering the road. Four serious-faced big- booted men were tramping down the road. Two in front carrying large bow saws. All were bare headed. '... a lorry there, last time...' we heard one mutter to the other as they passed. The two behind sported ear rings. One carried a long shafted axe.

'Gypos', they've a nose for decay,' I said, as we watched them pass.

'There're after firewood,' said Michael. And sure enough, stilled crouched in the hedgerow we heard the sound of sawing, the thwacking of an axe. Michael looked at us both, puts his hands out, palms up, 'told you.'

'Where're they going to put the firewood?' I said, after

a minute. Crouched down, we followed and saw the men throwing what they've cut up into the hedgerows either side of the road.

'Let's follow them down a bit more,' Frank said.

'I'll bet what happening here is that they're doing the cutting and a lorry will follow later, so it's not parked on the road, I said.

'Let's get out of here then before that lorry comes.' said Michael.

We reached the Culmore Road, stopped to catch our breath, check our shopping bags and cloth bags. All intact. We usually ran along the wall parallel to Culmore Road, crossed over into Troy Park through our scoot hole into our own territory. But we were tired. In addition, it was easier to run the short distance along the Culmore Road, than run behind the wall in a stone-strewn field.

.Laden with chestnuts, pears and apples, we ducked down as we entered our scoot hole. When we straightened up we heard, 'been shopping then boys, have we?' It was the same two policemen who'd let us go before.

'We've been here before, haven't we?' said the younger of the two policeman who'd not been keen to let us go the first time. The other policeman, who liked the sound of scoot hole, was right out of small talk. They must have seen us coming up the Culmore Road.

'I told you we should have stayed behind the wall,' said Frank.

One of them took the shopping bags. 'Keep you're cloth bag on, we'll see what's in them at the police station.'

They'd parked their police car on a house, driveway, set back off the road. We saw two people standing at their front door, watching as we were bundled into the back of the car. One of them was my music teacher Mr. Quinn.

They drove out of Troy Park and onto the Culmore Road

heading for the police station up at Waterloo place. The car's 'out of my way' bell sounded off. I looked at Michael and Frank, pointed my finger at the policeman who'd seemed OK. They both nodded.

'All the pears and apples in the shopping bags were given to us by Patricia Divvit.' Jason brought them up from the cellar. We helped Jason out in the orchard,' I said.

'Patricia Divvit is it now.' And Jason. We are well connected, aren't we,' said the scoot hole policeman.

I'll tell you what, he said, 'let's just drive down there and see Patricia and Jason and ask them.'

We all said OK

'The turning just ahead,' I said.

The younger policeman stopped the car and leaned over into the older policeman 'I think we should take these young rips up to the police station now. We've let them off the hook the last time. You're too soft with them.'

'We're going down to McDivvits. And that's an end to it Taggart,' said the older policeman.

'Listen, Sweeney, just because you're a...'

'Nothing to do with it,' Sweeney said. Make the turning, now.'

'Jesus Mother of God,' I thought. 'Sweeney'

Taggart cut the 'out of my way' bell. As we entered the private road to McDivvits we heard another bell ringing. A much louder bell.

'That's the bell in the bell tower at McDivvits,' I said. Something's wrong.'

'Sit back,' said Sweeney. We'll decide when something's wrong.'

Taggart drove slowly down the pot-holed road. All the branches and cut-up tree were in the hedgerows. It was about halfway down that we meet the slow-moving lorry. The lorry we'd seen with logs in it. But there were no logs in it now.

It was full of furniture jutting out through the white sheets roughly thrown over it

Both the lorry and the police car stopped, their engines idling. Sweeney got out. 'Bloody Gypos', we heard him mutter.

'Back up, back up,' he shouted, as he walked toward the lorry. Police business,' his raised arm and index finger pointing back.

Before Sweeney reached the lorry two of the men threw open either cab door and leaped out. The two in the back, who'd been steadying the load, leaped over the tail gate.

'That's Patricia McDivvit's lorry.' What are they doing with it?' I shouted across to Sweeney.

All four of the men scrambled through the hedgerow heading out at speed for the border and Moville. Sweeney drew his revolver, fired in the air. The huge thundering sound deafened our ears. Roosting crows flapped into the disturbed air their wings heaving.

The men kept running. Didn't even look back. Sweeney squatted down on one knee. Steadied his gun hand with the other and fired again. One of the runners fell to the ground grabbing at his bloodied leg. The other two kept going.

Taggart leaped out of the car. 'You three stay put,' he said.

Both lugged the bloodied man over to the lorry. Threw him in on the driver's side. 'Put her in reverse', Sweeny said, his .38 revolver still in his hand and now sitting alongside the wounded man.

Taggart climbed back into the car. He looked round at us. We were totally silent. 'Nothing to say then smart arse,' he said to me.

The lorry stopped maybe twenty yards from the house the wounded man's head no longer visible in the windscreen.

Taggart stopped the car, its radiator up against the radiator of the lorry. He dropped one of the windows, locked the car doors.

We heard the keening, wailing voice of Patricia McDivvit. I ducked my head out the open window. Blood was seeping out under the lorry door, dripping onto the running board. Taggart came back to the car. 'You, he said to me, out.'

I climbed out. He took hold of my arm and led me down to McDivvit's lawn. Sweeny was staring at the scene in front of him. His revolver still in his hand. He looked up at us. 'Stand clear,' he said.

Jason was lying full stretch in a pool of congealing blood under one of the chestnut trees. Fallen, burnished chestnuts, partially opened, lay in this stagnating pool. The axe I'd seen driven into the tree stump lay there too. Its silky shaft stained now with streaks of blood.

Patricia was on her knees alongside of him wailing, whimpering, the hem of her green, daisy-covered dress soaked in his blood.

'Are you Patricia McDivvit?' said Sweeny.

Patricia looked up and saw me. 'My son's dead John,' she said. They've killed my son.'

Sweeney turned around. 'She does know you,' he said.

Patricia's, her face and hair streaked with blood, her once bright mackerel, blue eyes opaque, fell on top of Jason wailing into his murdered back.

Sweeney woke up.' Get that man out of the lorry.' He tore off a length of cloth from one of the sheets on the lorry, rapped it just above the man's bleeding leg, jumped into the lorry, and reversed it down the side path.

'Get the boy back in the car. Reverse the car. There's a telephone in the shop on the Culmore Road, phone for an ambulance. Phone the station; let the Sergeant know what's happened. Keep the boys in the car. Go', said Sweeney to

Taggart.

Later, at the Police station I made a statement on behalf of my two brothers and me. Sweeney stayed with us as I did this. 'You get on home now, he said. I'd say nothing to anyone, if I were you. To you three the matter's closed. We'll deal with it from here on in. Leave the apples and pears, take the chestnuts.'

We made for the bus station on the Asylum Road. Sweeny gave us the fare. He wanted to walk us there.

'No, said Frank. 'Someone will see us with you. It won't matter to them that you're a catholic policeman.'

When we got home mother meet us at the back gate. 'Where've you three been?' I've been worried sick.'

We showed her the chestnuts.

The thing was here, which of us was going to tell father.

'Do you remember that night when mother broke down after our aunt found out we have blankets with arms,' I said to Michael and Frank.

'Yeah, so? Frank said.

'Didn't our aunt say something about her coming here every Saturday to re-assure father,' I said.

'Yeah, right,' said Michael. And father nodding his head in agreement with what she'd said.'

'That's right,' said Frank. I remember. It was all a bit odd that night wasn't it. The things our aunt said, father nodding in agreement.'

'It's just crossed my mind that what she meant was that she knew of Jason, she knew he was father's son and our half brother,' I said.

'Jesus Mother of God,' said Frank. You know I think you're right John.'

'And she just wanted to re-assure father that she'd not tell anyone about it, right,' said Michael.

'That's it,' I said. And as I told you on our way to Boom

Hall, she didn't want us to go near the house. Now we know why.'

After that Michael and Frank agreed that I should tell father. And that we none of us would tell anyone else. Not least in tribute to our dead aunt.

Father listened as I told him the whole story. Including our resolution. And the reasons for it.

'Now you know why I was saying 'sorry Mary', to your mother John, when Father Glakin was saying the prayers for the dying.' he said. He got up from the table, puts his hand on my shoulder, goes out the front door.

Next thing he starts to smoke cigarettes. Something he'd never done. And one night he came home drunk as a skunk. We three helped mother put him to bed. 'What's going on with your father?' mother said. I know you three know something. Tell me.'

His drinking didn't last long. He couldn't get a taste for it. But he kept smoking.

A few weeks later we read in the Derry Journal that the wounded man, one Neil McDaid, who'd made a full recovery, was charged with murder.

The story recounted that the men had gone quietly about stripping the house of its furniture. It was only when Jason and his mother heard the engine of their lorry start up that they became aware of what was happening.

Jason raced out and dragged the driver out of the truck. The others piled in to help the driver. Jason fought with them. But was no match for three. His mother came on the scene as Jason heaved the axe from the tree stump. One of the three men wrested the axe from Jason.

He fought the two in front of him, knocking one of them to the ground as his mother screamed at the men. But a brutal blow with the axe from behind finished him.

Both Sweeny and the other policeman got a

commendation.

Six months later, the Crown hanged Neil McDaid in the Crumlin Road prison for the murder of Jason McDivvit Boyle.

The Tiled Fire Place

Father knew his own trade, like he knew the face he saw in the mirror every morning he shaved. But he knew nothing about fitting fire places. My aunt Annie's, mother's sister, two sons were bricklayers, John and Billy, they did.

Now that our home had electric lights and sockets father thought it was time that our old range 'bit the coal dust'. I didn't want this to happen. Where was I going to put my chestnuts to toughen up?

We still had the gas cooker. I asked mother if I could put them into the gas oven. 'I'm not putting the gas cooker oven on for your chestnuts.' It was different with the range. Your father brought home a lot of timber from work. He doesn't bring gas home.' There was no way around this impeccable logic of mother's.

The two brothers, John and Billy told father that if he took the old range out on Friday, they'd come down and fit the new tiled fireplace on Saturday. That Friday, I called down after school to see uncle Fred.

'So your father's having a new tiled fireplace, fitted.' What was wrong with the range?' he said.

'I don't know, it beats me. Can I put my chestnuts in your range to toughen up uncle Fred?'

He slipped sixpence into my hand, 'Of course you can.'

Father took out the range on Friday night. The two brothers came early Saturday morning. The sun came out to greet them. They'd brought all the necessary materials in a lorry on loan from the Loch Swilly Railway Company courtesy of uncle Fred.

They set to work. Billy in the back yard mixing the mortar. John marking out the width of the new fireplace on the floor. Father hung back his hands in the pockets of his dungarees

I asked father if I could sit and watch.

'Sit quietly then and at the back of the room, so you don't get in the way.'

As the work went on and the sun got higher in the clear blue sky, the brothers striped to their simmets. Outside of both these, hung around their necks, were two brown scapulars, one to the back, and one to the front. And a miraculous medal each that shone on a thin silver-like chain.

As they worked they talked endlessly. As I remembered my sisters doing. But Billy and John's talk was worth listening too. They too had card schools in their back lanes. From what they were saying these almost always ended up in an argument or a fight with bloody noses, black eyes and cracked ribs.

'Did you know Joe Ferry?' I said to Billy.

Father looked over at me with raised eyebrows, his lips pursed.

'Sure we know Joe,' said Billy. If he'd played cards as well as he'd boxed he'd be in Las Vegas playing now.'

'Las Vegas, what's that?' I said.

They both laughed.

'Sit back there John,' said father.

'He's alright Johnnie, there's no harm in him,' said Billy.

They talked about the parish priest coming into the back

lane to try to persuade them to stop playing cards. How'd they'd stood listening in respective silence to the priest's tirade. Then getting back to their cards as soon as he'd gone.

'Was his name Father Glackin?' I said.

Then the police, snooping around the back lane, and all the card players going utterly silent when questioned.

I fell silent at this mention of the police. On and on they went about other champion bricklayers, they were working with at the Du Pont Maydown Plant in the Waterside.

Father, who'd been watching Billy, was now mixing the mortar. Around ten o'clock he made a brew of tea using the gas cooker and the big kettle. He poured the boiling water into a delf teapot and wrapped a tea cosy around it. A tea cosy, not something you'd see on a building site, prompted Billy to say, 'What's that around the teapot Johnnie?'

'Pay no attention to him,' said John. He' just taking the...' he looked at me... the pee.'

Father poured the tea into three big mugs. Hands me a cup. Now that they'd stopped working I wondered if they'd stop talking as well. But not a bit of it. They'd no sooner settled with their tea than Billy, winking at John said, 'We were all sorry to hear about your sister Gerty. She was a lovely woman.'

Father nodded his head, took a sip of his tea. Said nothing.

'Left everything to the McDivvits daughter.' I'll bet you wondered a bit at that Johnnie,' said John.

Billy, nodding his head, said, 'I'll bet.'

'Yeah', well...' father said as he had a gulp of tea. He lit up a cigarette and looked out into the back yard. John and Billy weren't going to let this rest. It was almost as though they consented to fit the fireplace to glean a bit of family gossip. Especially about the McDivvit's daughter.

The more I saw the unease in father about this line of

conversation the more unease I felt. I now began to wish that John and Billy would end this McDivvit thing. But that wasn't going to happen.

A sort of dull silence fell. I watched father. He started to fidget with the bib of the braces on his dungarees. A slug of tea, then another puff of the cigarette, another look out the back yard. Father's fingers, stained a deep dull brown, although he'd not long started to smoke

'Bit of a free spirit, wasn't she, the daughter?' Especially when it came to men and stuff',' said Billy smiling and winking at John.

'Ay, well,' said father, shrugging his shoulders, stamping out his cigarette, it takes all kinds.'

'Must have made you wonder though Johnnie leaving everything to McDivvit daughter,' said Billy.

'Not everything,' said father, as he swigged the rest of his tea and stood up. 'She left the house to St. Vincent De Paul. There wasn't much money left to leave either.'

Father turned as he made his way out to the yard, 'I'll get you some more mortar, no rush on you, finish your tea,' he said.

Father was never much of talker at the best of times. I knew why he didn't want to talk about his dead sister, or McDivvit's daughter. And the shock that Michael, Frank and I had when we saw Jason, took a bit of getting over as well.

Late afternoon, with the new tiled fireplace, fitted, the brothers cleaned their trowels as father and I tidied up. Father made another brew and he and the brothers had a final mug. I got a second cup.

'I heard McDivvits daughter's getting married,' said Billy as he supped his tea.

Father, got up from where he was sitting and looked at him 'Oh yeah', he said. 'Who too?'

'The older of the two policemen, a man called Sweeny

who found her son, after the gypos had finished with him. He lives in Messines Park, just up the road from you.'

'Thanks for fitting the fireplace,' father said, shaking both their hands.

'No problem Johnnie.' Leave of the lighting of the fire until tomorrow morning. Let things settle,' said Billy.

The next morning, mother and we children all gathered around the new tiled fireplace as father prepared to light the fire for the first time. Crumpled pages of newspaper, axed timber sticks and a few bits of coal sat waiting in the unstained iron grate.

Father used the same device he used to get the fire going in the range. A two-foot long piece of half-inch copper tube, pierced with numerous holes for a foot of its length. He connected this to a flexible hose, which he pushed onto the serrated gas tap. The same tap used for the gas iron.

He put a match to the paper. Slide the perforated section of the copper tube under the paper and turned the gas on gently. There was a whoosh', as the gas ignited and aided by the draw of the newly built-in flue it was blazing in a matter of moments.

At the whoosh' of gas mother looked across at me and give me a half smile. The smell of gas lingered in the kitchen for a little while.

But I stilled missed the old range. I loved to spit on the red-hot lids and watch my spit blister and skitter into steam. Can't do that with the tiled fireplace. Just as well I'd made a deal with uncle Fred to put my chestnuts to harden and toughen in his range which he'd sensible not taken out. Although mother compromised in that she allowed me to put my chestnuts in the gas cooker when she was baking. But only then.

For the next few weeks after the fitting of the new fireplace, father, home from a long day's work of ten hours, worked every evening making and fitting new cupboards in the recesses either side of the new fireplace. Then he came home with a radio. He plugged into one of the new electric sockets.

From then on, every Wednesday night we'd all gather round to listen to Orson Wells and 'The Black Museum'.

This began with Well's deep sombre voice, his slow footsteps echoing along the dark corridors of the Black Museum, the chimes of Big Ben, as he talked about items, an axe, a razor, a knife, that had been used in an actual murder.

The first night we all sat and listened, father had switched the electric light of, entranced and terrified. And right in the middle of when Well's was explaining the gruesome details of some wicked murder, father rattled the thin plywood doors of the new cupboard and we all collapsed in terror and laughter. For the first time in months, I saw my father smile.

When later on we got our first black and white television, well that was something entirely different from the innocence of the radio. Plays in 'Arm Chair Theatre' on the BBC, in the late 50', were socially realistic dramas grounded in my own experiences.

Once and only once, I encouraged everyone, including mother and father to watch one of these plays. The shock came about half-way through. One of the men characters was trying to induce his girlfriend to go to bed with him.

This was enough for mother and father to look at me with raised eyebrows, pursed lips. And those raised eyebrows, pursed lips, were quickly followed by, 'Turn that off, now,' from father, when the girlfriend said, OK, I'll go to bed with you, but I'm not taking my knickers off'.'

I looked across at Frank, he was squirming in his seat, his face bright red. He jumped up and ran out of the kitchen into the scullery. Nobody else said a word. After a few minutes I followed Frank out. His face still red, forehead plastered with perspiration.

'What's up Frank?' I said.

He told me that anything at all to do with sex talked about in public put him into a state of panic, made him blush until his face was on fire.

'The other day,' Frank said, 'I was sitting playing cards with some of my friends. One of whom starts to talk about sex, homosexual sex. I felt this panic coming on, my face started to flush, my forehead sweat.'

'What'd you do?' I said.

'As it's happened quite a few times, I've learned a new trick to deal with it.'

'Tell me Frank,' I said. I feel uneasy when I hear talk about sex as well.'

'I found if I talked instead of listened, I could handle it.'

'For Christ's sake Frank, tell me?'

He told me that in this particular instance when the talk was going to be about homosexual sex, and before it really got going, he said to the guy, 'Well, I suppose your story is going begin with, 'once a Pounce a time'.' That got a burst of laughter. And took the pressure off me.'

Having thought for a minute about Frank's strategy for avoiding overwhelming embarrassment I said, ' I remember Brian Friel, one of my teachers at school, he use to say that intelligence, 'is what we do when we don't know what to do'.

'Yeah?' Frank said. You think?'

In any event, the girl saying that she wasn't going to take her kickers of brought to an abrupt halt the whole family ever watching 'Arm Chair Theatre'' again.

In 1957 Billy and John Sweeny died. Both killed in a bus crash on their way to work at the DuPont Maydown Plant in the Waterside. A foggy morning. Speeding drivers. Their side of the bus ripped out by the force of the crash. The bodies identified by the scapulars, the miraculous medals.

Mother took me to the wake at 'The Glen'. I remember the two black wreaths on aunt Anne's and Uncle Fred's front doors. The long desolate wail of agony from my aunt as my mother hugged her. Trying to console the inconsolable.

'My two sons,' she wailed. My two sons. Jesus, Mary and Joseph, Mary, why they. They were so innocent. They'd never harmed anyone. If they'd been married with children I'd have had something, something...'

On and on she went. With neighbours and family members crowding around her, reaching out, touching her, stroking her. But, she wasn't to be consoled.

Uncle Fred sat silently in his chair, his head bowed in front of the range fire. He'd the same poker in his hand as he had when Ann and I were there while mother was having Michael. He was poking and hoking at the dying embers of the coal. The knob of the poker even more worn. The business end, more twisted, more tortured.

I went up to him and put my hand on his shoulder. He turned, lifting his head and looked up at me. His eyes were opaque. His face expressionless. He shook his head a little. Then turned back to poking the fire.

Half way through the solemnity of the rosary, my aunt again, lifting her head up, let out a long inconsolable wail.

It was some months later I asked mother if I should call down and see uncle Fred at the Lough Swilly station. He was back at work again. Uncle Fred was standing upright in his oiled-stained boiler suit mechanically wiping the windscreen of one of the Lough Swilly buses. The poker I saw him poking the range fire with was in the long, narrow ruler pocket of his dungarees.

'Uncle Fred,' I said. He looked round. His eyes still dead. He pushed his mouth back in a brief grimace. I walked up to him. Not sure what to do. But knowing somehow that it was what I had to do, what I wanted to do.

'How are you John?' he said. He carried on wiping the windscreen. I started to cry. Not loud. But crying. He turned toward me. Dropped the cloth and knelt down in front of me. He reached out and pulled me into his arms. I smelt the oil from his boiler suit. His breath, harsh in my face. His grip tight.

Another man, in a similar oily boiler suit, crossed the yard towards us.

'All right Fred?' he said.

Uncle Fred got off his knees. 'This is my brother's young son John.' His voice broke as he said, 'young son John.' I'm just going to walk him home. I'll not be long.'

We walked together up the Buncrana Road, past St. Patrick's chapel. I looked up at him as we passed. He didn't bless himself. Nor did I. The light breeze stiffened. Squally rain whipped our backs.

Carefully opening the gate that was falling off its hinges, the 'shoemaker's children being the worst shod' we walked up the concrete path to our front door.

I didn't like to tell him we never came in by the front door as it was thought of as unlucky.

Although mother and I did when coming home from the pictures.

'You tell your mother, John, to tell her sister, I'm sorry,' he said as he pressed a sixpence into my hand.

He knocked at the door and turned back down our path. I watched as he eased the gate back after him and turned to go in the opposite direction to the Lough Swilly Train depot.

I looked down at the sixpence in my hand. It was worn, defaced, thin. As I watched him go, the sixpence fell from my hand. In a daze, I saw it blown down the path across the pavement and into the road drain. There to be buffeted, pitched and tossed past St Patrick's chapel and spun into the river Foyle and on out into the harsh uncaring Atlantic Ocean. Mother opened the door. 'Uncle Fred brought me home,' I said.

'Good, good,' mother said. Where is he?'

I pointed up the Buncrana Road. We both looked to see him turning into where we played football on Saturday. 'What's he doing going up there?' mother said.

As she spoke, the Lough Swilly train's whistle blasted out its shrill uncaring shriek. It was the last train to go out of the Lough Swilly Train station on its way to Buncrana before the company closed down. It was all buses after that.

Dan O'Hara, painting the goal posts that day, said he saw Fred enter the pitch. He watched him as he made his way up to the gate leading onto the railway line. He followed as it was unusual to see anyone else in the field with no football match going on.

Uncle Fred had climbed the gate. Walked up alongside the railway lines. Stood there, taking what looked like a poker out of the narrow pocket of his dungarees As the train approached, he held the poker up to the driver waving to him. The driver waved back. Fred threw the poker aside, stepped in front of the train.

Starting Work

Fast asleep that first morning I awoke to a hand shaking my shoulder. It was father. It didn't seem as though five minutes had passed since he shook my shoulder for school. My two brothers were snoring. I got out of bed and donned my new flannel shirt, flannel trousers, and carrying my new thick-soles shoes, quietly left the bedroom.

When mother first presented me with my new work flannel trousers, I told her I didn't like them. 'What's that mean?' You don't like them.'

'The legs are too wide.' Can't you take them in?'

'You mean you want to be a 'Teddy Boy', even going to work?' She did a cracking job of taking them in.

The coal fire in the new tiled fireplace threw shaky shadows across the kitchen. On the table, breakfast a boiled egg and two slices of buttered toast. Father was already eating his. The silence, but for the hissing and the flaring of the burning coal, was in sharp contrast with what it was like when the whole family was at the table. But I was all for it.

Father sported a shirt and tie, a pair of dark trousers and polished thick soles shoes. His dungarees and my new dungarees were in a green canvas bag alongside the table. Two tin lunch boxes sat on the table. Father's battered and scarred. Mine brand new, smaller. We left the house at 6:30 am and made our way to the bus stop opposite Messines Park a few hundred yards from our home. The buses having finally got beyond the British Navy Base at the bottom of the Buncrana Road.

We climbed off the bus at the Guildhall. Walked along Foyle Street, up St. John's Street and along the Abercorn road. The streets were quiet but for a group of maybe twenty men standing at the top of St. John's Street.

'They're corner boys,' father said. 'The same kind of "tossers" who play pitch and toss and cards in our back lane.'

Coming to Abercorn Road we saw women, in groups of threes and fours, shoaling towards us dressed in blue one-piece uniforms, chattering away, with a burst of youthful laughter echoing through the early morning street. I wondered who, and where they were going.

The men started to whistle and shout at these girls. 'Are you coming out tonight with me Mary Rafferty', said one. 'No, said another. She said she's coming out with me, didn't you say Mary?'

The women largely ignored them. They were corner boys. 'Get yourself a job, standing there, sucking on your Woodbine. Bloody corner boys.'

'Go home to your Mammies,' said another.

'Like the trousers,' one of the women in front shouts at me with a big smile of her face.

Father looked across at me. His eyebrows raised, the makings of a smile crossing his face. She saw I was like her, going to work. Her hair was pitch black, big white teeth like an open piano. I looked after her. The slow swing of her hips reminded me of my sitting on a horse and cart and watching the sway of the horse's hips.

That night I asked mother. 'They were heading for the shirt factory, Tilly and Henderson's on our side of the

Craigavon Bridge,' mother said.

'They were all women; don't men work there as well?'

'No, she said. 'And I should know because as a young woman I worked there. Making shirt cuffs and sewing together men's shirts.'

I couldn't image mother making shirt cuffs. I wondered if she'd made the shirt cuffs of the stranger, I'd seen in our scullery scrubbing his big hands in our Belfast sink.

The concrete floor of the workshop was cold underfoot even with my new thick soles shoes. Six benches similarly constructed as father's, but wider and longer, sat impassively along the length of the workshop.

Eddie Hughes, the shop foreman, white aproned, was cutting up bits of short ends of timber on the band saw and throwing them along side a big cast-iron stove. The stove already lit, its lid glowing red, had a big tapering iron pot with a long ridged handle on it. The rotten-egg smell coming from it told me it was pellets of animal glue melting.

Hughes picked up this pot and took it to a small stove at the back of the workshop. He scooped a big black swan-necked kettle, like the one we have, from the floor and handed it to me. 'There's a water tap outside, Johnnie boy,' he said. Fill her up.'

I looked around to see if father was behind me as I thought he was talking to him. He wasn't. Hughes was talking to me. I filled the big kettle up and plonked it on the red-hot lid of the stove just as I'd seen mother do on our old range. Some of the water spilled out skittering across the lid of the stove.

I heard Hughes says to father, 'What's your young fella got on his legs Johnnie?'

That first morning I just largely wandered around the workshop from bench to bench. 'Pass me that saw Johnnie,' one of the men said as I went by his bench. 'Take hold of that,' said another. During the first day, I got to understand

131

what the phrase 'dour apprentices' meant. And I was to see the next five years as one.

'Don't do it like that, do it like this.' That's not how I told you to do it.' Are you never going to learn?' I wanted to be encased in a suit of armour to protect me from this, 'don't do this, don't do that, do it like this', regime.

It reminded me a bit of when mother use to say to me as child, 'shss, shss.' I'd hated that 'shss'. And later learned to hate, 'don't do it like that, do it like this' with the same passion.

It wasn't long before I was asking myself, 'What is all this? What am I doing here? What does this have to do with anything of any importance to my life?'

I just didn't see the point of it at all. I just wanted to be back in my streets, tearing through my shortcuts, dodging into my scoot holes. I was as easy in my streets as the otter is in water. I was master of my own little universe. This all stopped when I went to 'Work'?

I felt like a machine that anybody in the workshop could switch off or on without a bye-your-leave. I was ablaze with energy, completely absorbed in myself. I didn't want anybody but me to switch me on or off.

There was a big circular saw at the bottom of the workshop. When it first started up I jumped, banging my knee on one of the benches. The buzz of the planer was softer, with chippings hurtling out of its mouth as it cleaned the rough-sawn timber the circular saw cut.

By midday the area around the circular saw was deep in different coloured sawdust. Around the planer, timber chippings littered the concrete floor. Motes of sawdust, caught in a weak sunbeam fusing through one of the sawdust-coated windows, floated in the air. I started to sneeze. I spent the rest of the day sweeping these up, and bagging them.

And as we at home left the Brock out for the pig man,

so too the sawdust and chipping were left outside for the pig man. He'd spread them on the floor of his sties.

When I got home that first day I fell asleep at the kitchen table. Tired out with the non-stopness of the day. Someone must have carried me to bed. Five minutes later I felt father's hand shaking my shoulder again.

I enjoyed watching father working with his tools though. But I didn't enjoy my days in the workshop. Mother, and others, told me that I was lucky to have an apprenticeship. Yeah, right. And so I'd no choice. I just had to get on with it. Which in the end, I suppose, I'm glad I did. As a tradesman, I've always been in work. But I don't think I've ever got over the initial shock of it all. And the loss of who I once was.

Another morning Hughes sent the yard labourer, Danny, and me down to 'Keys' timber yard on the Strand Road. We were loading timber onto the handcart when one of the office staff shouts out. 'Are you Johnnie Boyle, McLaugh and Hall? There's a telephone call for you.'

I'd never used a telephone. Barely knew what one was, never mind answering one. The guy in the office hands me the telephone. I put it to my ear. The guy catches my eye, twirls his index finger around as he lifts his eyebrow. I reverse the phone

I heard this noise in the phone. 'What?'

'Is that you Johnnie?'

'It's me', I said.

'Bring a long stand back with you from Key's. And a bubble for a level.'

'How many long stands do you want?' And is one bubble enough?' I said, waiting for the next move in the game. I might not have used a phone before, but I knew codology when I heard it.

Another time in Keys, Danny, who had a bit of a stutter, took the phone. The office staff and I watched. I thought I heard Hughes's voice at the other end. When Danny tried to answer back his stutter took off good style. He couldn't get out one complete word. His big face grew redder and redder. Sweat dripped from his brow.

After a few minutes of this I head Hughes's loud guffaw at the other end of the phone. Danny slammed the phone down. 'You shower of...' The office staff held their sides. Hughes knew of Danny's stutter. And knew that it just got progressively worse when he was on the phone.

The office staff knew this too. 'Jesus Mother of God,' said one, he falls for it every time.'

'Cruel buggers,' I thought.

One day I watched father running a piece of timber over the top of the planer. However it happened, his hand, flat down on the piece of timber, made contact with the spinning blades of the planer. I watched him as ran this piece over, dropped it, closed his hand into a fist, and raced out of the workshop. Twenty minutes later, he was back.

'Are you all right, Johnnie?' Hughes said.

'Ah, I'm OK.'

Watching I saw him showing the palm of his hand to Hughes. Little pin pricks of blood dotted each of his fingers and palm. Hughes pointed to the sawdust beside the big circular saw.

Father squatted on his hunkers and settled his hands into the sawdust. After a minute, he went back to the planer and started it up again.

I watched as he ran the edge of the timber over the planer. Then he dropped one end onto the concrete floor and closing one eye, sighted down this edge. He saw me watching. 'You know why I do that?' Before I could answer he said. 'To make sure it's dead straight.'

'You learn something every day,' I thought.

As father was sighting down the edge of this piece of

timber a voice behind him said, 'Would you like me to sight down that for you Johnnie?'

Father told me later that this guy was the boss's brother, Tony McLaugh.

Father looks and winks at me. He hands the piece over to Tony.

'Watch this Johnnie boy,' Tony said. He grabs hold of the piece and starts to sight down it. He puts his index finger and thumb up to his eye. I thought, he's pulling a mote of sawdust out of it. But he wasn't. He's only popped his eye out of his head and was now running it along the edge of the board. He'd a glass eye. A bit of comic relief here. Sorely needed.

One morning the workshop took delivery of a two handcart loads of desktops. These from St. Columb's College a hundred yard or so further down Bishop Street and directly across from the Nazareth House, the home of the Nuns of the 'Sisters of Nazareth'.

'Hey Johnnie boy,' Hughes said to me. Take out all the ink well, check, and remove drawing pins, chewing gum, whatever. We don't want the planer blades blunted now, do we? Make an even worse mess of your 'Oldman's' hands.' I'd never heard father called ' Oldman' before. It was a term of affection I was sure.

With these desktops now ready for the planer, father pushed them through and I caught them at the other end. I couldn't believe how the planner transformed them. They were dull, dark with harsh raised grain. But once through the planner they emerged silken, fresh, a deep burnished brown, shot through with lighter strips of coloured grain.

They reminded me of the chestnuts I'd got at Boom Hall, each a burnished brown jewel. The pungent, sweet forestry smell of the chippings took over the workshop for days afterwards. Pitch pine. 'A real timber' father said. The pig man's pigs were in for an aromatic treat.

Turns out Jack McLaugh, our boss, owned the pig farm. And the bacon curing factory next door. Sort of like him having all his pigs in the one basket.

Another apprentice started a few days later. Peter something. I didn't catch his last name. Hughes was his uncle. I heard him complaining to Hughes on his first day that he couldn't stand the noise of the machines.

And that he didn't like the smell of the sawdust and shavings. He stood around that first morning dusting himself off every time some sawdust or chipping landed on him.

At our ten o'clock brew, I said to him. 'I can't believe you don't like the smell of the pitch pine at least.' And what about how the desktops come out of the planner, transformed.' He was not even remotely interested.

'Don't want to know. Not interested. I told Mummy I didn't want this job in the first place.'

The last time I used 'Mummy' I was three.

'You don't think you're lucky, having an apprenticeship?'

'No, I do not', he said. And if you've any sense you'll get yourself out of this as well.'

'Tell me about it.' I said. I'm told I should be over the moon having this job.'

'Well, he said, you're over the moon on your own as far as I'm concerned.'

'How're you going to get out of it?' I said.

Come lunchtime Peter squatted down and threw both chipping and sawdust all over him to convince his mother just how dusty and dirty it was in the workshop. He wasn't back the second day. The next we heard he'd a job in an insurance office. 'Sensible lad he,' I thought.

There was another Boyle in the workshop. Alex Boyle, who took over when Hughes retired. Boyle's wife had given birth to two stillborn babies. Both boys. The boss, Jackie

McLaugh gave him permission to make two coffins for his dead sons in the workshop. Beautifully shaped clean oak, adorned with brass handles. French polished, lightly sanded, French polished, lightly sanded five times.

The lids of the coffins had counter sunk brass screws. Boyle drove them home as a priest from the 'Long Tower' chapel blessed both coffins, sprinkling holy water over them. We all stood in silence, including McLaugh.

Father not only worked in the workshop but also travelled around various sites for McLaugh and Hall. He worked in Marlborough Road (where Brian Friel used to live) on a housing site. When I was at Rosemount School, I used to call over to see and eat with him, listen to music, sneeze sawdust from my nose.

We both worked at St Marys School in the Creggan Estate just up from the Rosemount School. I spent two years of my apprenticeship there. After we'd both been there for just over a year I went up to one of the other men. Before I could say anything, he said. 'You're Johnnie Boyle's young fella, right?'

'Right, I said. Is my Oldman always this quiet, I mean I've never seen or heard him talking to anyone. Even when we're on a tea or lunch break with the other men.'

He looked at me with raised eyebrows, a puckered grimaced mouth. 'You've been here for a year and as far as I know, I'm the first man on the site you've spoken to in that year.' You're a chip off the old block,' he said.

I told him I didn't mind being a chip off the old block so long as that block was pitch pine.

Working at St Mary's school in the Creggan Estate and after our midday break, all six of we apprentice would stand outside and watch the girls pass on the way home for their one hour break from the Rosemount shirt factory. We looked better and were more privileged than the corner boys were.

What chances they, after being turfed out of the 'Secondary Schools' that were supposed to teach them a trade. These schools were supposed to swerve away from an exam culture. Help the less academically inclined to find fulfilment in a trade. But they' simply ignored these pupils. And spent their time in giving those thought capable of passing the 11+ a second time, an academic 'leg up.' The rest dumped onto our street corners. There to fester and seethe, cannon fodder for the coming years. The vast majority of us, who became apprentices, were 'grandfathered' in as I was by my father.

I'd a trade. I stood there in my dungarees. Brass-caped ruler sticking out of my pocket. A hammer stuck in my belt. Pencil behind my ear. I looked like I was going places. Well, in comparison to the corner boys anyway. I'd whistle and call after these girl like the rest. The girls paid attention. A trade stood for something in Derry in the fifties.

Then when I'd meet one of these girls somewhere else the ice was broken and I'd 'get off'' with her. You'd have thought that with all the sisters I have, getting on with girls would be a cake walk. Well, it wasn't.

One reason was that at fourteen, my face was covered in acne. Not exactly an inducement to the girls. But I did meet up with one of these girls from the Rosemount shirt factory. Sylva, would you believe, in a city of Maureen's, Ann's, Bridget's... I meet a Sylva. She was about fifteen stone. I was nine and a half. She lived on Sackville Street. I used to sit on *her* knee. I could feel the heat of her. It was like sitting on the workshop stove.

During my apprenticeship, I also worked at St. Columb's College, just opposite the 'Nazareth House', home of the 'wee Nuns' as some affectionately knew them. Standing under the eaves of the College roof repairing a rotted window sash, I watched a youth called out by a tall, stocky priest.

From deep in the pocket of his soutane he drew out, like a gun from a holster, a double-stitched leather strap. Soutane billowing he lashed the hand of the offending pupil until it was red-raw. All the while the bent heads of all the other pupils scribbling frantically into their exercise books. Talking to one of the pupils later, he told me this strap they called a 'Cloaker'.

But working there as a 'hewer of wood and carrier of water' I knew I'd missed out on something important. And what had I missed out on? The 11+ exam. When I'd asked father what this 11+ was? He'd said, '11+ what?' C'est la vie.

Years later, father used to take me to football matches in the 'Brandwell' in the Bogside. It was here that Joe Ferry my brother-in law, had set his mind to race his newly acquired greyhounds.

Seamus Heaney, the Irish poet, when boarding at St. Columb's College in the fifties, and looking down into the Bogside said he was, ' Looking down into the inflamed throat of the Brandwell'. An inflamed throat, further inflamed by the then 'Secondary Schools'.

Working, at the 'Nazareth House' one day, easing a few doors, fitting a pane of glass I met this young girl. I was sitting eating my lunch, scone bread with sultanas – mother's speciality – when I heard this quiet knock on the door where I'd just fitted the pane of glass.

I pulled the door open. She stood there with her head bowed. I went back to my seat and continued to eat my lunch. 'What's your name?' I said. She slowly entered the room. Looked quickly behind her and closed the door quietly.

'I'm thirty nine,' she said. She didn't look more that my age of fourteen, her hair jagged as though cut with garden shears. She lifted her bowed head and looked straight into my eyes. Her eyes widened. She moved slowly towards me.

Put her hands on my face and stroked my cheeks.

They smelt of disinfectant. Like the smell in mother's bedroom when I was three. And the smell of the old mattresses we'd got from St. Vincent De Pauls. She moved her hands to my head, stroking my hair. Something left my heart and entered my throat. I stood up. 'You look different,' she said.

'Different?'

'You're like me,' she said. What's your name?'

'John.

'No, she said. 'Your number. May I have a piece of your bread please?' I handed her a piece. She pushed it into her mouth and swallowed it in one go.

'Your not thirty nine years old,' I said

'Thirty nine's my name.'

She sat down beside me. 'What day's today?'

'Tuesday, I said.

'They tell us stories on Tuesday. I don't like them.'

'What kind of stories?'

'Last Tuesday it was about a coach and horses jammed full of weeping lost souls being driven to the devil by a roaring screaming madman along the Lecky Road at night. He's lashing the horses with a long black whip. The Nun said the crack of the whip was the sound of a soul breaking in two.'

She stopped. Almost out of breath. She got up and turned towards me. 'Will you take me away from here John?'

I looked at her. 'Would you like another piece of soda bread?' My mother bakes it for me.'

As she put the second piece of soda bread up to her mouth the door swung open. A young plump Nun with a long white scar across her top lip, barrelled into the room, tore the bread from the girl's mouth. She looked me as though I were some kind of diseased rag.

'Out, she said, now.' The girl bolted from the room.

The same Nun came back a few minutes later. 'There's a telephone call for you, on the hall phone.'

'Hello,' I said.

'Gather up your tools Johnnie boy. Come back to the workshop,' Hughes said. That was the last time I worked there.

But I never forgot the girl who thought her name was 'thirty nine'. Nor the plump Nun with the long white scar across her top lip.

Joe and Ann

My sister Ann, at the fifteen – spitting image of mother – had a boyfriend. Joe Ferry, an amateur boxer, joiner, milkman, handy man, and a Crown-kept breadwinner. His 'Oldman' had an interest in a cowherd in the Irish 'Free State'. The Ferrys' lived in a big private house in Park Avenue, Rosemount not far from the Rosemount school.

Ann thought she'd landed on her feet running when she first met Joe. This simply because of where he lived. And had a job. Jobs for men in Derry in the 50's were as scare as horses' toes. Joe's family had both property and a business.

Although Ann looked like Elizabeth Taylor, Joe didn't look like Richard Button. But he had one thing in common with Burton. Burton's capacity for the consumption of alcohol

Joe had small peevish looking alert fisherman's eyes. His wormy mouth, when open, showed stained and irregular teeth. He talked from the side of his mouth. Smoked Park Drive cigarettes the cheapest brand on the market.

Ann, at fifteen, worked in 'Tilly and Henderson' the shirt factory on our end of the Craigavon Bridge at the top of Saint John's Street. She was happy in her work and used to say she loved having her hands inside men's shirts before they did.

When Ann first met Joe she was reading the 'Red Star' romantic magazine. A 'Mills and Boon' read. I used to watch as she clasped it in her hands pouring over it, head down. She saw this magazine as a guide to what married life held for her with Boyo Joe. This notion was as about as safe as entering politics straight from a convent.

When Joe first came to call, he was met at the front door by father. He sized him up. How was he dressed? Did he look shifty? Was he working? But with Joe, father was more lenient in his sizing up. Even though he saw just how shifty Joe looked at that first meeting with those runt-like peevish eyes. And the fact he talked out of the side of his mouth.

'Ann tells me you live on Park Avenue.' Is that right?' father said.

'That's right Mr. Boyle and we own a herd of milking cows in the 'Free State' as well.'

After this mother took over. Joe then made, heart-felt representations to her about his feelings for Ann. Only then did he gain entrance to our front room parlour where mother made sure Ann and he had to themselves – for fifteen minutes anyway.

Then the rest of us piled in to see Ann's new boyfriend. Not having heard the name of her new boyfriend, I didn't expect what I now saw in front of me. And I don't think Joe expected what he saw in front of him.

'Hi Joe, I said. 'Still playing cards and punching men in the back lane on a Sunday?'

Ann hearing this turned and said, 'I didn't know you played cards Joe?' You never told me that.'

Joe looked at me with those little peevish eyes of his. The same look he'd given McDermott before he floored him in the back lane that Sunday.

'I used to play Ann, but I don't any more.'

'Are you still boxing Joe?' I said.

I showed Joe my mouth organ that father had bought for me when he saw how I listened to the music on his little portable American radio.

'This will tide you over.' he'd said. It'll be a little while until you can join St. Columb's band with McDaid.'

'Give it here and I'll play you a tune,' Joe said.

I handed it over. He played 'Danny Boy'. I was impressed. So was Ann. Which was the whole idea. He then asked me to play a tune. Ann nodded to me. 'Go ahead John,' she said.

I liked Ann. Because, not only did she look like mother, but she also excluded girlish warmth in the way she smiled with both her eyes and mouth. Anyway, I drew the mouth organ up and played 'The Soldiers' Song'.

'What tune that?' Joe said, looking across at Ann, a smile, if not a smirk, on his little ferret-like face.

'The Soldiers Song, I said, surprised at such a stupid question. Our after-school Irish teacher taught me to sing it. 'Soldiers are we, whose life we pledge for Ireland... Some have come...' I sang in a low voice. 'You mean you don't know 'The Soldiers Song Joe?' I said, looking at Ann as if to say, 'What sort of boyfriend's this you've got, doesn't even know the Soldiers Song.'

'I know the Soldiers Song alright,' Joe said. But that's not what you've just played.'

Joe was out to get his own back here. He didn't like my mentioning in front of Ann that I knew he played cards and knocked people out in back lanes.

'You pay no attention to him,' Ann said. He thinks he knows everything because he lives on posh Park Avenue. Don't you Joe.' However, she smiled across at him all the same. Park Avenue written all over her smile.

I started not liking him then, at all.

'You're just blowing into that thing and making a noise. The tune's in your head you gom.'

I'd heard that word 'gom' before with its implied notion of 'stupid'. This was hard to take. And it was something I never really forgive Joe for. I saw from then everything about him with a jaundiced eye. A jaundiced eye that carried my opinion of him to the right conclusion.

'When you were playing cards Joe, why'd you come the whole way from Rosemount down to Pennyburn to play?' I said.

'Well, I'm not playing cards now that's all that matters. Right Ann?' he said, turning to smile his sly Park Avenue smile at her.

All this brought to mind a little episode that happened when I was about four years old. I'd had this really clear dream about a dog. A small lively black and white terrier. I named him Danny. We were running through tall grass. The sun was shining. The sky cloudless and blue. We raced together along Buncrana beach, across the ribbed sea sand. I dived into the warm flat water. Danny followed. We swam out to a small sandy Island. But the weather turned around. The wind stiffened. The sea became rough as storm clouds gathered. Danny started to bark...

The next morning, when I woke up I asked Ann where my dog was. Ann was puzzled. 'What dog John?' she said. You've not got a dog.'

And there was no dog, yet it was all so vivid, so real. I could still smell Danny. Hear him barking as storm clouds gathered. In remembering this now, it crossed my mind that maybe Joe was right about my mouth organ playing.

That it was all like the dream of the dog in my head. And that I was as he'd said, just blowing into it and making a noise, but hearing what I wanted to hear in my head. He'd a knack of confusing me this Joe boyo.

Maureen, who'd been sitting quietly listening to Joe and me playing the mouth organ said, 'Hey Ann, you remember the little tapes in a round box that aunt Annie used to sometimes bring down on a Sunday after Mass?' You remember?' she said. Bit like John playing the mouth organ. Don't' you think?'

I remembered those tapes as well. And caught where Maureen was going with this. Father McIntyre, a first cousin to our aunt Annie, ordained as a priest, went to Africa, Nigeria, on his missions. Every once in a while he'd send home to aunt Annie little recordings of his singing of Irish Ballads. These included Danny Boy and the Soldiers Song.

We'd all sat hushed in wonder. We'd never seen or heard the like before. A voice coming from a little box. But after about five minutes of listening to Father McIntyre it was obvious, even to our cloth ears, that he couldn't sing for two pence. But he thought he could. Or imagined he could.

There was a bit of crackling, fair enough, but we could barely make the words out. Or even get a sense of what song he was trying to sing. We only knew what song he was trying to sing as he told us before he started to sing it. He sounded a bit like Father Glackin would if he tried to sing, after having more alter wine than was good for him.

After this encounter with Joe in our parlour, I next saw him at his wedding when he married my sister Ann. There was a brief honeymoon in Buncrana. Then later, a Corporation house in the Creggan Estate, where Aishling and Irene were born. Two beautiful girls, looking just like their mother. Thank God for that at least.

Before Joe married Ann I saw him once in action in a boxing ring. He was a boxer not a fighter. He danced around, bobbing and weaving. His favourite punch the kidney punch.

Which he delivered with lightning speed and accuracy. At this particular fight, his opponent looked a lot heavier, to my untutored eye anyway. This other guy was a fighter. No bobbing and weaving for him. He just stood his ground. And ever now and then he'd sock Joe hard. Joe kept firing lefts to his ribcage, pounding the guy's face. But he just came back for more. And once in a while, socking Joe so hard you'd have heard it in the Bogside half a mile away.

In the end Joe won. Someone, no one knew who, distracted the referee. Joe punched the guy below the belt, followed up with a further savage punch to the crotch.

I'd called up once to see Ann in the Creggan Estate. The front door was open. Ann was lying on the floor, curled up crying. I picked her up and put her on the settee. She was clutching her side. One of her eyes swollen purple. There was no sign of Joe.

'Where's the girls?' I said.

'They're in their room. They ran up there when they saw Joe hit me.'

'Why in God's name did you marry that 'tosser' in the first place?'

'Jesus Christ, John,' she said. I was sixteen. What did I know at sixteen?' He's a carpenter like father. His family owns their own home on Park Avenue, for God's sake. Not the bloody Bogside or the Creggan Estate.'

'Well, you're in the bloody Creggan Estate now, good style now Ann,' I said.

The next time I called up to see Ann was when I'd heard that Joe had bought two greyhounds. He was sitting at the table playing a game of cards with another man. There was no money on the table. He upped his head at me. 'Dan, he said, this is Ann's brother.' Dan upped his head at me as well.

'How are you John?' said Ann coming in from the yard. Aishling, who'd been playing outside came running in crying.

'Billy Curran hit me in the face Joe.' Ann had told me both Aishling and Irene always called him 'Joe'. Never Dad or Daddy

Joe, throwing his cards down, jumped up knocking his chair over. 'Where's he now Aishling?'

'Don't Joe, don't,' Aishling said.

We followed Joe outside. Four boys were kicking a ball around. 'Where's Curran?' One of the boys stepped forward. Joe socked him in the face with a right, then a left to the kidneys. The boy crumpled to the ground moaning, clutching at his side. 'Touch her again – any of you – and I'll leave you on crutches for the rest of your miserable life.'

'Joe, Joe', Ann said, as she gripped his arm. He elbowed her away.

The next time I met him, I was a supervisor on a building site in the Waterside in Derry. The site boss, from Donegal, whom we called 'Packy', was looking for joiners. The Crown sent Joe out for an interview. His morose face and worn-thin lips creased into a knowing, half-baked smirk when he saw it was it was me.

'Listen John – that's your name, isn't it? He said. As if he didn't know. 'The story here is John; I'm delivering milk for the old man. And I've got a few other bits and pieces up and running as well.'

Joe had more bit and pieces, 'up and running', than ten men playing pitch and toss.

'I don't really want this job,' he said. I'm alright where I am on the Crown. Just fill in the form, saying, I'm not suitable. I just don't want a full-time job. I'd be no use to you here.'

I knew that one of the other 'bits and pieces' Ferry had up and running, were his two experienced racing greyhounds bought recently with the proceeds of his milk round, his 'foreigners', and the Crown. From St. Columb's College, you can look down into the inflamed throat of the Brandwell in the Bogside. And it was here at the Brandwell greyhound track, that Joe was to race his two hounds for the first time when the season started.

In the meantime, he fed the hounds on the best of everything. Better feed and looked after than Ann and their two girls. When they were in the house lying in front of a blazing coal fire, Joe kept their muzzles and blinkers on. A big fine-meshed fireguard caught the smallest of sparks before it reached them.

'For God's sake, Joe', where are we to keep two bloody greyhounds?' said Ann when Joe first told her.

'In the back yard.'

'What about them barking?' said Aishling.

'They don't,' Joe said.

The two girls were at first cautious with the hounds, but stroked their fine delicate heads. 'Why have they that thing over their mouth Joe?' Irene said.

'They're only muzzled now, not when they're on the race track,' Joe said.

'Why's that?' Aishling said.

He looked at them both. 'They've got to know they can kill the hare. They won't know that if they're muzzled.'

'Why do they always have those things either side of their heads?' said Irene.

'They're called 'blinkers.' With those on, they only see the hare in front of them, nothing else. I always keep them on when out walking them.'

Joe had built a wall and a floor insulated shed with soft pillowing for the hounds to lie on, their thin skin leaving them vulnerable to the cold. 'These two hounds are our future,' Joe told them. I can make more money here than I ever did at anything else. Including boxing.'

The only money Joe ever made at boxing was when he'd throw a fight for a betting trio of hard men from the Bogside or the Creggan Estate. Ann knew why Joe went into boxing.

An outlet for his violent temper. She hoped the greyhounds would be this outlet too. Joe called one of his hounds 'Boxer' and the other 'Ref'. As though he too hoped the same.

Ann and the two girls were at first bemused at Joe's infatuation with the two greyhounds. They'd listen to him talking to them. Whispering their names, stroking them. He'd be up in the middle of the night to check on them. He'd feed and watered them twice times a day, every day. Take them for long walks every morning. Jogging with them on the way back.

Soon the two girls were as infatuated as Joe was. Whispering to them just like Joe. Ann looked on with fingers crossed that Joe's temper had found another boxing ring. He started to take the two girls out with him when he walked the hounds. Joe always kept both the hounds blinkers and muzzles on when out walking.

'Can't we take their muzzles off when they're in the house?' said Irene. But Joe would have none of it. They were in the house for two hours each day.

'Here Boxer', said Aishling encouraging the hound to leave the fireplace and place its long legs on her knees as she stroked him endlessly. Joe looked on. When the two hours were up Joe puts them back in the hut.

'We don't want to spoil them, do we?' he said. They're hunting hounds. Working animals. Not pets.'

A week before the first race, Dan Doherty, from whom Joe had bought the hounds, called round. Joe had arranged with Dan to take the hounds out from now on until the first race. Joe and he had struck a deal. Ann could see that.

She didn't ask what. Joe told Ann he'd other business to attend to. But he told her he and Dan were to take both hounds to the Brandywell race track a few days before the race to let them get the feel of the track. And give them a trial run. Dan and the two girls took the hounds out for their last walk before this run at the Brandywell. The two girls were walking behind Dan.

'You ask him,' Aishling said. It's you who thought of it.'

'Dan likes you better than me,' said Irene.

'So?' said Aishling.

They walked on in silence. Both hounds trotting along nicely their bright muzzles and blinkers glinting softly in the weak sunshine.

'Dan,' said Aishling.

Dan turned round, but keeps walking.

'Can we stop walking for a minute?'

Dan and the hounds stopped.

'This is our last walk with Boxer and Ref'. What do you think of taking their muzzles and blinkers of' for us?'

'Why', said Dan

'We've never seen them with their muzzles and blinker off at the same time?' said Irene. I'll bet they'll look even more beautiful.'

Dan started to walk on. The girls followed. 'Aw well, at least we tried,' Aishling said.

Dan heard this and stopped again. 'Well, he said, 'if I take their muzzles off I'll have to leave their blinkers on so as they don't see anything they shouldn't.'

Dan told them he knew a place, not far from where they now were, that would be great for the hounds to prance about without their muzzles. But only for a little while.

Both girls, smiling at one another, said together, 'Thank you Dan.'

As they entered the lane they usually went down, Dan stopped and opened a big field gate. They all went through. 'I know the farmer who owns this land. He won't mind. There's no stock or crops or anywhere like that near. And the hounds will only prance about a bit. I'll do them good for when they go to the Brandwell racing track with your Dad and me tomorrow.'

'Hold the leads girls,' I'll take their muzzles off,' said Dan.

He knelt down in front of the greyhounds, loosened their muzzles and eased them off. Both hounds immediately shook their head from side to side and started to prance up and down. Just as Dan had said they would.

'Just look at those heads, now their muzzles are off, aren't they a sight,' said Aishling.

They're beautiful,' said Irene. I wish we could keep their muzzles of all the time.'

Aishling held Boxer's lead. Irene, slightly ahead of Aishling, holding Ref's. Dan all the time smiling as he looked at both the hounds and girls enjoying themselves. He'd never seen either the hounds or the girls so content as this before. And he was at the house regularly playing cards with Joe.

After about five minutes Dan said, 'Right girls, time to put their muzzles back on and head for home.' As he bent down to put the muzzle back on Boxer a hare bounded across his vision.

Boxer leaped forward, tearing the lead out of Aishling hand and bolted past Dan. Aishling let out a scream. Ref now saw the hare and he too yanked the lead out of Irene's hand and tore after Boxer catching up with him. Now the two hounds, neck and neck, raced Helter skelter after the hare. This was not the trial run intended.

'Jesus, Mother of God', said Dan as he now raced after the hounds leaving the girls lagging behind. Dan had now lost sight of the them. He continued running, the sweat pouring off him. His heart pounding. When Aishling and Irene caught up with him, he had his hands on his knees, bent over, sweat dripping from his forehead, his face a deep red.

He was gulping air into his lungs. The girls stopped, catching their breath. They waited for Dan. 'Where's Boxer and Ref?' said Aishling as Irene took her hand. 'Where's Boxer and Ref?' Dan lifted one hand off his knee and pointed. 'Behind there,' he said, putting his hands back on his knees. Aishling and Irene moved forward to where he'd pointed. They were on the rock almost before they saw it. It ran at a right angle to them.

A foot in from where the rock began both Boxer and Ref lay. Their fragile, beautiful heads smashed to smithereens. Aishling and Irene came back to Dan. Both were crying and hugging one another. 'What happened Dan?' said Aishling.

Dan was now standing upright. His arms by his side. His head on his chest. 'The hare leaped over the rock, the hounds, at full stretch, didn't see it. They only saw the hare.'

Dan took the girls home. He told Ann what happened. 'Let me know when Joe's home. I'll come round and talk to him. I'll go back and have a word with the farmer. We'll sort things out.'

'Where's the hounds, are they in the shed?' said Joe. Then he saw Aishling and Irene huddled together on the sofa. 'What's wrong with the girls?'

'The girls asked Dan to take the muzzles of the hounds. They wanted to see what they looked like without them. The hounds saw a hare. They went after it. They're dead Joe,' Ann said.

When Joe hit her, he hit her professionally. As though she were in the ring with him. He fired his right twice in quick succession in Ann's face. Then a left to the right side of her ribcage. A liver punch. Ann fell backwards, crashing to the floor. She didn't move. The two girls were screaming. But Joe wanted them to see.

Years later when the two girls had grown up and left home, so did Ann. The farmer Dan knew owned some cottages at Cosh Quinn just before you come to the border with the Irish Republic. I used to pass there on my way over the border to pick up pipe tobacco for father. She's still there.

The Strike

I'm lying in the boot of Nigel McCormack's stopped car. He's winding down the window. I hear the raucous voices of hard men. 'Is all them Fenians of the site now Nigel,' one of them says.

'All of them,' says McCormack.

'You'd wonder at the likes of you, working with them in the first place.'

'I work for our friends at the Londonderry Corporation.'

'Well, our friends in the Corpy are out on strike as well.'

'Off you go. We want our own to finish these houses, not a bunch Fenians,' he says.

McCormack winds up the window and drives slowly down the unmade site road. I ease the boot door up. Seven men, all carrying pickaxe handles, one with a Lee- Enfield bolt-action rifle over his shoulder are all gathered in a tight bunch, like pitch and toss players, their backs to us. As I watch, they split into two groups of three as they start to search the houses either side of the road for any stray Fenians. The one with the Lee-Enfield rifle stays put, hunkering down on the unmade site road.

John McDermott, a local hotelier and lawful guarantor of 'Derry Construction Ltd' picked up the tab when the firm went bust. This before the completion of twelve public sector houses in the Waterside.

McDermott made contact with Harry Doherty from the Bogside in Derry who'd drawn up the Bill of Quantities for the job. They meet at the 'Collon Bar' in Pennyburn to discuss terms. McDermott, who'd taken the 'Pledge' didn't like meeting in a bar. However, Harry insisted. McDermott, as an hotelier, had scant knowledge of the building trade. Harry agreed to manage the site for him

The upshot of this meeting was that, two weeks later, fourteen men, all from the Irish Republic landed on the deserted site. Joiners, electricians, painters, labourers, all crammed into a long-wheel base Ford van, driven by 'Packy, the new site foreman, a friend of Harry's.

Neither Harry nor Packy knew Nigel McCormack, the Clerk of Works designated by the Derry Corporation. Harry petitioned the Corporation to have another clerk of the works installed, one whom he knew, but to no avail. They made it clear that their choice of Clerk of Works stood.

McCormack, an ex British serviceman, lived in Messines Park, a three-minute walk from where I was born in St. Patrick's Terrace. He lived there with other ex Servicemen. The Derry Corporation built the houses for them.

These ex Servicemen were both catholic and protestant. They'd fought at the battle of Messines in Flanders during the First World War. The Catholics for one reason, the Protestants another.

I knew McCormack having delivered the 'Belfast Telegraph' to him in Messines Park, when I had a paper round. He was a keen clarinet player. Being a Protestant, he played a different tune to my Catholic one. It was he who told me that Packy was looking for another joiner, cards in. A week later, I was knocking up stud partitions and hanging doors on the site in the Waterside.

All the houses were ready for the second- fix trades. The site didn't look, or feel, any different to any other site I'd worked on. Except that every day, but Friday, and without fail, there have been always one or two men missing. Some days three or four men would be missing. And, some days, there'd be only six men on site.

I asked Packy about this. 'I've got them doing some work that Harry's priced up in Derry City' They'll only be gone for a week or two. Don't worry about it.' Every Friday, all fourteen men were on site.

Early each Friday morning John McDermott arrived on site with the week's wages in a small locked black suitcase. He'd spend about three hours on site, going around with both Harry and Packy, checking on the progress of the work.

He'd talk to the different tradesmen, asking them what they thought of how the site was coming along. They always had a ready answer, primed by Packy. Any major queries he had, he raised with Harry. He always had a plausible answer too. McDermott would leave the site at around eleven o'clock, taking his small, empty, black suitcase with him.

Harry had one of the houses that looked down the unmade road to the entrance of the site, converted into temporary offices. One for Packy, on the ground floor, one for Harry on the first floor, with the side front room (what mother called the parlour) for McCormack.

Now and then, I would sit with him when having a brew. He was a Jazz fan too. And, a bit of storyteller as it turned out. I told McCormick once what Father Glackin said about Messines Park and how Catholics and Protestants had fought together in the First World War.

Father Glackin felt that there must have been some camaraderie between the Catholic and Protestant troops. How else could they fight effectively? And that it was a great pity indeed that the camaraderie that they brought back with

157

them, now seemed lost.

I also mentioned the names of the two boys, Edgar McBride and Nigel Sweeney, from Messines Park, with whom I'd made my first communion.

'Do you know those two boys?' I said.

' I don't,' he said. But I know they live in Messines Park.'

McCormick, like Father Glackin, knew that Catholics and Protestants had fought at the battle of Messines in Flanders. 'For different reasons, for sure,' he said. The fact remains that Derry men, both Protestant and Catholic fought together on the same side in the First World War, and it's a tragedy that they are at one another's throats now.'

'As a Protestant you'll know that I've no time for catholic saints', McCormack said, a half smile of his face, but your Glackin sounds like one in comparison to a Presbyterian minister I once knew.'

He told me the tale, about this Presbyterian Minister. He was the genuine article bible thumper. Hell's fire and brimstone, where his constant and only theme. His parishioners loved him. He put the fear of God, not only into them, but into their children too. He'd have put the fear of God into a block of concrete,' McCormick said.

This Minister had a writer friend. This friend gave him half a dozen books on modern Irish writing. It was a transformation. He packed in his Ministry went and got himself a job with the B.B.C. And, started to write himself. And became quite good at it.

Years afterwards, he returned to his parish to see his dying mother. His parishioners came to him in droves. 'We thought you were the greatest preacher we ever had. We sorely missed you.

'We loved they way you put the fear of God into us and our children. Are you never coming back?'

Without the slightest hesitation, but remembering the six books of modern Irish writing, he'd been given all those years ago, he said, 'Too many books spoil the cloth.'

On a practical level, as well as a storytelling level, McCormick taught me to use a 'dumpy' level laying out the road curbs on the site, after I'd asked Packy if it was all right to do this. He had the nod from Harry, who didn't like McCormack. The upshot was that a few weeks later Packy made me up to site supervisor. I shared his office.

One day, when Packy was out of the office, the phone rang. I picked it up. 'Hello, John Boyle, site supervisor.'

'This's the Department of Social Services.'

Social Services what do they want?

'We'd like to call over to the site and inspect the 'National Insurance Cards' of those working on the site.'

'Why, I said, looking at Packy as he came back into the office, holding the phone with one hand and pointing to it with the index finger of the other. 'The Crown,' I mouthed at him.

'Just routine', the Crown said.

' When?

'How about this Friday at eleven. It's Wednesday now, gives you few days notice, OK?'

'Hang on, ', I said.

'What's all that about?' Packy said.

'The Crown, they want to come out and check on the number of National Insurance Cards as against the number of men on the site this Friday at eleven.'

'Tell them three o'clock would suit us better,' Packy said.

'See you at three o'clock this Friday then,' the Crown said. There'll be three of us, get it sorted quicker that way.'

'I'd better tell himself,' Packy said, as he made toward the stairs to Harry's office.

Harry made contact with me after I'd arrived on site at eight that Friday morning. He came into the office and said to Packy, 'Can you spare John for a bit, I want to have a word to him.'

'Right, Packy said, as though he'd been expecting this.

'I thought the drawings you did for the kitchen units were well detailed,' Harry said. And I like the way you got McCormack to show you how to use the dumpy level. Useful if he's off sick. Or something happens to him.'

I'd done technical drawings at the Strand Road Technical College. And I'd made up drawings to show the construction of kitchen units and their location within the kitchen

'You live in Pennyburn don't you?' said Harry.

'Half-Pennyburn, I said. I told him about 'money-bags' Father Glackin. He laughed at this.

'You're Johnnie Boyle's boy, aren't you? I know your Oldman, and two of your sisters, Bernadette and Eleanor, right? I'm pleased Packy made you up to site supervisor. And knowing your family means I can trust you, right?'

'Right, I said.

'I heard one of Packy's lads was whinging to you about his pay packet.'

'Well, I said, he asked me if I my wage packet had details of my tax and national insurance contributions.'

'What did you say to that? Harry said, as we dandered along the unmade site road.

'I told, him, I didn't talk about stuff like that. That it was my business what was in or on my pay-packet.'

'Right, Harry said. What's his name?

'I don't really know, but I heard the others call him Seamus.'

He told me he'd just recently been to Lourdes. 'Seen the light, he said. I was jack the lad once, but after that visit to Lourdes... well, it just totally changed me. Now, I'm as straight as an arrow.'

He then went on to tell me he'd convinced Packy to go to Lourdes as well. And that when Packy was gone it was important to him that he had someone else he could trust on site, right?

As we sauntered along, we met McDermott entering the site carrying a small black suitcase. Walking towards us, he bent to pick something off the ground.

'See, he said, as he held up four wire nails, 'this is where all my money is going. And I just passed three or four bits of copper pipe lying in the road as well.

You'll have to put a stop to this waste Harry.' He looked at me. 'Who's this?' Harry told him. 'Hmm, he said. 'What's this about a visit from the Crown?'

'That's all in hand, it's not a problem. I'll be up in a minute, John, Packy's in the office,' Harry said.

He then turned to me and said, 'What's your view as to how we deal with these men from the Crown Johnnie, when they come.' Calling me Johnnie now. 'Buttering up' good style going on here,' I thought.

I told him I'd been on the Crown for about six months before starting here. That I'd been doing a lot of foreigners. I needed the extra money having four mouths to feed at home. And that one morning queuing up to sign on I saw the woman behind the signing-on desk was the same one I'd been working for the previous week. I'd said to the lad in front of me, whom I knew, Mickey Sweeney, 'That's the women I was doing a foreigner for last week.' She'll know me straight away.'

Mickey turned to me and said 'Keep your shirt on Johnnie boy. The guy I'm doing a foreigner for is the Manager here. Just sign on as usual, no sweat.'

Sure enough, the woman for whom I'd been doing a foreigner, looked straight at me. 'Next please,' she said, without batting an eyelid.

I'm Irish, but told I'm British. Had the majority offer a little good will towards this notion of my being Irish it would have made things so different. This is how we Irish Catholics felt. This sense that we'd been stitched up and that made taking the Crown's money a no brainer.

'Nonetheless, I said to Harry, 'I'm happier working cards in, as here. It keeps my state pension up. And I'm not looking over my shoulder all the time. There's always one smart arse Crown snoop out trying to catch you working on the 'Q. T.'

Harry listened to this without interrupting. Then he said, 'Packy and I have talked about a visit from some such snoops. This is why we've laid on a bit of a surprise for our friends from the Crown. They're here at three o'clock this afternoon, aren't they? We'll see them coming onto the site from my office. Be there before three, right.'

At around three o'clock, with McDermott, and his little black suitcase well off site, we three were standing looking out of Harry's first-floor office window. There was a clear view of the unmade road leading down to the site entrance. Harry's brown brief case lay on the desk.

Three men, black suited, ambled onto the site walking alongside one another as though for support. Each carried a big hard-backed book, like my site dairy. Out of one of the houses, either side of the road, two of Packy's men came.

Each of the four was carrying a pickaxe hand. We watched the suits stop, look at one another. They knew it was time to 'fish or cut bait'.

There was maybe a hundred yards between them and the four men. One of them looked up at us. Packy raised his right arm and threw it forward. With a collective roar the pick-wielding men speed down the road towards the suits their pickaxe handles thrust in front of them.

Three hardback books 'bite the dust' as the suits scrambled back to the entrance of the site, piled into their car and screeched off. Harry and Packy looked at me, waiting for some comment.

'Some surprise,' I said, as I nodded my head.

Shortly after this, I took a phone call from McDermott. 'So, he said, how'd the visit from the Crown go?

'All sorted Mr. McDermott, no problem.'

"Good, he said. We don't want any trouble with the Crown, do we?'

'Absolutely not Mr. McDermott,' I said.

'Right. Put Harry on the phone...' what's your name again?'

Around four o'clock, we three were again standing in Harry's office. 'Do you know what's in the black suitcase McDermott brings to the site every Friday? Harry said.

'No, I don't.

Packy locked the office door as Harry opened his brown suitcase, dumped the content onto his desktop, and spreads it out. Pay packets, fifteen in all.

'This is what was in McDermott's black suitcase,' Harry said.

'Why only fifteen? Where's your and Packy's?

Harry told me he and Packy had their own special arrangements with McDermott.

Each of these pay packets showed an employee's name, the net amount due after deductions for National Insurance and Income Tax. Harry opened a drawer, took out a clear plastic bag, and dumped the content on the other side of his desk. More pay packets, each showing nothing.

'Packy's off on holidays shortly for a few weeks. I told him we could trust you, right? Harry said.

'Right, I said. Where're you going on holiday,' I said to Packy, as if I didn't know.

'Lourdes, he said.

'When Packy's in Lourdes, I'll need you to help me, with what Packy and I are going to show you now,' Harry said. He rummaged through detailed pay packets, picked out mine, and handed it to me.

'There'll be more than that for you next week, Johnnie.'

And as you can see from your pay packet your income tax and national insurance deductions are up to date, keeping your State pension intact,' Packy said.

Is there anything these two haven't thought of?

Packy opened all the detailed pay packets and started taking out the cash. He placed this money alongside each pay packet.

Checking with each pay packet, as he goes along he takes out the National Insurance and Income Tax. As he does this, Harry is writing the names of the employees' on the empty pay packets.

'So this is what the previous 'buttering up' is all about', I thought.

Packy returned to each pay packet and deducted another thirty pounds from each. He saw me looking at him. 'Well, he said, 'it's only fair. I bring them to work each morning and get them back at night. And it's only fair, that, as they're all signing on the Dole in Buncrana, and miss a day each week on site, that we deduct something for that. See what I mean?

'Sure', I said. I see what you mean.'

Harry then went on to tell me that he's other work for these lads in Derry. These lads are paid extra, in cash.

'McDermott's watching pennies as his pounds whizz past him', I thought.

Harry then places all these cash deductions and the now empty detailed pay packets into his brown brief and snaps it shut. What's left Packy places into the pay packets that have only the employees' names on them.

'As you'll have guessed Johnnie,' Harry said, Packy and I split this money between us, in the 'Collon Bar', in Pennyburn where I first meet McDermott. He hates coming in there, so we're not likely to run into him. And as from next week your share will be an extra seventy pound a week, on top of your wages. And you can help me organise the other work we have in Derry, bit extra there too, all cash.'

'What do you think of that?

'Great, I said. 'That's fine. Roll on next week.' I thought about Seamus, who'd asked me about my pay packet's details. And how after I'd told Harry I never saw him again.

'As you see Johnnie, Harry said, 'it's all less money for the Crown. It's no different from you signing on and working on the Q.T. at the same time. You see that, don't you?

'I see that,' I said. But I wasn't so sure about this as Harry was, thinking this is way beyond my working on the Q.T.

Harry picked up his brown briefcase, looked at his watch. 'It's four thirty, let's have a brew,' he said. Nip down Packy and put the kettle on.' Packy nips down the stairs we follow, the electric kettle's singing when we entered Packy's office on the ground floor.

As we drank our tea, looking across to the cement hut we could see through the open door the men doing the same.

The first gunshot shattered the big front window of Packy's office. 'Jesus, what was that,' he said. There was no question as to what it was when a second shot whistled over our heads. A third shot ploughed through the cement hut. Out of the cement hut, men, bent low, raced across to Packy's office where his transit van's parked.

"I'm out here', Packy said, as he flew out of his office and leaped into his van that was now full of men shouting and swearing

'For Christ's sake Packy, get us out here.'

Harry ran out after Packy and jumped into the front of

the van. He leant out the window and shouted at me. 'Stay here Johnnie, I'll send help.'

'Wait', I shouted back, wait.' I grabbed Harry's brief case, flew across to the van all the while shouting at Harry.

Packy was revving the accelerator. I pulled open the back of the van, throwing Harry's brief case in among the men. 'Open it,' I shouted.

The van bounces off down the unmade road. McCormack came out of his undisturbed office, hands raised in the air. He sees me. 'My car's round the back get in the boot John.'

Pacemaker

Years later, multiple other bedtime pleasures, knotted binders notwithstanding, now accompanied the more prosaic pleasure of my spinning, dizzy head. Something I've had since early childhood.

Prosaic or not though, I remember the satisfaction I got in bed when I flung my head back on the pillow and something inside my head spun around at a terrific speed. I saw little stars, shinning, bursting in front of me.

When this first happened, it frightened me. I thought I was going to die. But gradually I began to enjoy it. I'd fling my head back, close my eyes, and feel my head spinning like a whipped top.

That was my only pleasure in bed when I was very young. Father Glackin having put paid to any other pleasures with his 'impure thoughts and acts' regime. And his confidence in the knotted binder preventing these 'impure acts'. I.e., preventing me rolling onto to my back.

Not that I've ever tried it. But you hear so much about it these days. And see so much about in films, that I should image that the glorious head spinning sensation I got when I flung my head back on the pillow, was the equivalent of using a 'Class A' drug. This drug, equally addictive, yes, but not free at the 'point of delivery' (as we say about our 'National Health Service) as was flinging my head back on the pillow.

But this time around the spinning and dizziness was different. And the difference came utterly unannounced, like a freak of winter sunshine glancing of a hillside. I'm standing talking to my wife on the phone. It falls from my hand. I look at it lying there. Then I collapse onto the floor with it.

I didn't exactly fall, it was more like I slow-motioned to the floor my head feeling as though it belonged to someone else. A barrage of pulsating flashes of strobe lighting, my eyes at a 'rave party'.

My heart was hammering like a boot in a washing machine, my hands shaking at the speed of light.

None of my spinning, dizzy heads had ended like this before. They just seemed to evaporate after a minute or two. But not this time. 'What's this?

'What's this? I heard myself say. Then, 'Get up you soft mutt.'

But I couldn't get up. And didn't pass out completely either. Whom it was wanted to get up and who it was couldn't I didn't figure out, at the time.

Later I remembered the run on the Buncrana beach when I was three year's old. I'd left my footprints and hand prints in the ribbed sea sand. I now realize that it was 'I' who wants to get up and it was 'me' who couldn't. And the 'me' are my foot and hand prints in the sand. They couldn't get up either.

At the Cardio-Respiratory Department, an external heart monitor picked up an abnormal heart rhythm. Yet this abnormal heart rhythm was something I'd contended with for donkey's years without this falling down business. The upshot was that I'm to have a 'pacemaker' fitted.

The buzz-saw sound of lawn mowers, the pervasive smell of newly mown grass lying in frail bundles, greeted me as I entered the hospital grounds.

A Health Care Assistant approached with a small shaving razor in her hand as I lay, pyjama clad, in a ward bed. 'I'll have to shave your chest before the operation.' she said.

Not having seen my chest hair, she didn't realise I'll take a lawn mower for this. A past holiday photo highlighted a profuse white fungus that is my chest hair. I cut and shaved it off then, but not since. And with my man 'boobs' and pronounced nipples I thought... 'Would you mind if I did that,' taking my pyjama top off and reaching for the razor. She thrust the razor into my hand, catching sight of the silvery jungle of matted hair.

Just before my operation, I had a short visit from the Head Cardiac Surgeon. 'Good Morning, 'I'm Ms. Swanson. How are you feeling?'

Ms. Swanson, a tall, woman, early fifties, with eyebrows that never stopped, had come round to give me a bit of a pep talk. She was re-assuring and informative.

I didn't get any specific details of the operation, except that it should take about half and hour or so. Titanium alloyed with aluminium are the metals used in the making of a pacemaker, making it extremely strong and light, I'm told.

This was just as well. Six months into having had it fitted, and doing a bit of DIY at home (timbering out the kitchen ceiling) I smacked the pacemaker full on with the claw of my hammer.

The hammer fell from my hand. I stood stock still, waiting for the fall. It didn't come. All down to the titanium the A&E doctor at the Hospital told me as she examined the deep purple bruise directly over my intact pacemaker. She'd never heard of, or seen, a pacemaker hit with a claw hammer before. She thought it something novel and amusing.

'Chest looks good,' said Ms. Swanson as she left.

I'd thought that Ms. Swanson would be carrying out the operation. But she wasn't. It was a much younger Cardiac Surgeon. He looked about twenty-one.

Bright and breezy. Probably Ms. Swanson's apprentice. Do they have apprentice surgeons? Yes, they do. I've just met one.

'A local anaesthetic is all you get for this job,' he said.

' Oh, I said. 'I am disappointed. I thought I'd be getting a whiff of gas. I like the smell of gas.'

He seemed amused at this. Well, we're off to a good start here if I've got the surgeon amused even before he begins his work.

'Sorry to disappoint, he said.' We only use gas as a General anaesthetic. It knocks you out completely. As you'll feel little, or no pain, you'd don't need it.'

'Well, there you go. You learn something everyday,' I thought.

Lying flat out I saw a small black and white T.V. monitor directly in front of me. Only it didn't look like any T.V. screen I'd ever seen. For a start, the picture didn't move.

'Lets you watch the whole show,' said the surgeon.

'Is that me?' I said, not having my glasses to hand.

'I hope so,' he said.

'Can I have it in colour?'

'It's in black and white for a reason,' he said.

'Don't tell me what that reason is.'

After the initial banter, and in calm, authoritative voice the young surgeon tells me what he's going to do to me over the next half hour, or so. He sees what he's going to do to me on the same small black and white T.V. monitor I'm watching. So, we're all set and singing from the same T.V. screen

After splashing my entire chest with an antiseptic liquid, the young surgeon's going to cut my chest open near my collarbone. Then push two steel wires, (hopefully stainless) one at a time, through my veins and into my heart.

Watching the monitor screen, he sees exactly, where the steel wires are going. Sometimes one wire is enough. I'm having two – but not by request.

One wire's pushed through my vein to the top chamber of my heart (atrium) and one wire's pushed through a second vein into the bottom chamber of my heart. (Right ventricle) 'When do I get the anaesthetic?' Is it a necessary part of the procedure for me to watch?'

Not as it turned out to matter whether my watching was part of the procedure or not. But I did get a local anaesthetic. As soon as it kicked in the cutting started.

Unlike when I first started falling down, but not passing out, here I just passed out completely ten minutes or so into the operation. I awoke to hear the surgeon's voice as he's watching the T.V screen.

'These aren't the leads (steel wires) I asked for Get me the ones I did ask for.'

'There're the only ones we've got, as well as being the ones you asked for,' said the nurse.

'Well, they aren't the right ones, I can't get them through.'

I heard something thrown across the room.

'Oh, hello, I'm sorry, I must have fallen asleep,' I said. My eyes were stinging. Someone had lit a fire on my chest. The nurse wiped the sweat off my face.

I looked up on hearing a hammering noise above me. Dust was falling from the encased, vibrating florescent lighting

'You didn't fall asleep,' the nurse said.

I recognise her voice from, 'Well there're the only ones we've got.'

'You passed out.'

171

'How'd I do that?'

'Pain,' the nurse said. Her frankness was somehow reassuring.

Along side me blisters of speckled blood dotted the tiled floor, like red coins of different dominations. Some glistening, others dull and congealed.

'We're having a bit of a problem with the leads.' But don't worry, we're going to get this right,' said the surgeon.

He leaned over me again, looking at the monitor. Sweat was cascading down my face. My tongue felt like the dropped gangplank of a cattle truck. I fell asleep. When I awoke, I lay still and quiet. This was not a problem.

'It's my lunch break now,' one nurse said.

'And it's my half-day.' I should have been out of here an hour ago,' said the other.

'Ah', said the surgeon, you've with us once more.'

'Did I fall asleep again?'

'I'm afraid it's all taking a bit longer that first thought.' he said.

I hear a door open. Ms. Swanson entered the theatre. The young surgeon moved away from me. And what looked and sounded like a heated exchange took place. I caught the tail end of Ms. Swanson's '... much longer.'

'How're we getting on now?' I said to the surgeon.

He told me he, finally, had the wires into position and that all that now needed doing was to plant the pacemaker in my chest.

His hand begins pushing and pressing the pacemaker into my chest.

After a bit, a good bit, I looked up. His face was red with exertion, perspiration building on his forehead. He wiped it with the arm of his gown before one of the nurses could.

I remember wondering vaguely at the time why he didn't just get up on a nearby chair and stomp the pacemaker into my chest with the heel of his shoe. I begin to feel sleepy... I thought, 'I'm going to pass out again and this time I'm not going to wake up.' Panic gripped me, sweat stinging my eyes, a black hole opened up above me. It sucked me in.'

'Don't panic,' the nurse said. 'Don't panic.'

I forced open my eyes. It's the 'frank' nurse. She wipes the sweat from my face.

'Don't panic. It's over now'. Time to break out the buntings,' she said, looking steadily at the young cardiac surgeon, his red face reddening further.

He looks at me. Turns the palms of his hands up. Nods his head as I say, 'You should have given me a whiff of gas after all.'

CPSIA information can be obtained at www.ICGtesting.com
Printed in the USA
LVOW10s1510210716

497248LV00016B/541/P